"No Regrets"

©Copyright 2019 by Monya Williams

For information address

ISBN: 978-1-7338763-1-5

Cover photography: ©Monya Williams

Printed in The United States

"No Regrets"

By
Monya Williams

Dedicated to those who sacrificed in helping me be the best that I could be. Thank you for helping me reach my level.

No one can live your life for you. Not every decision you make or choice you make will be the right one. But it is up to you to decide if the one you made is right for you. Love comes in many forms and many truths. Only you can define what Love is. There will be ups, downs, turns and round-about. There may be some tear shedding and heartbreaks but be wise they are all lessons. Some good, some bad but lessons nonetheless. Many may not understand your choices that's because they don't understand your heart. Those in your life will have various opinions about the choices you make. Your voice is the only one that should be heard. Your love, your life, your choice, your pain, your happiness, your light beloved it is all you. Even when you feel foolish for loving someone who didn't love you back. Know that it is within them and nothing you did or didn't do.

Peace and Blessing Beloved,
∞ Monya Williams ∞

No Regrets

Prologue

There comes a time in one's life where one may have to come to some understanding and I think mine is now. Just the other day I was on the internet trying to find a nice jazz cd when I must have typed in the wrong thing because up pops a picture of my hearts joy and pain. We shared a love that was so true and pure. See Sabrina and I grew up together and were always friends. Good thing sleeping together didn't destroy that but made our bond much stronger. I can remember a few years back when I saw her, we looked into each other's eyes and it was as if there was no one else in the room. She walked over to me and gave me a hug with such love in it I almost melted. We smiled at each other then fell out laughing. See the thing with us we never had any bad blood but our lives just went into different directions. I knew there were things in her life she wanted to pursue. I knew if I had it my way, she never would have followed her heart. Some times when loves comes knocking you have to make some sacrifices. Mine was to end a lovely relationship so she can become the woman she always dreamed of and if it's meant to be we will be once again. I never wanted her to put her life on hold in order to make me happy. I knew at some point she may resent me for it. I'd rather her resent me for giving her a choice rather than taking something from her.

Sabrina made it very easy to love and be loved so I never wanted to cage this kind of love. She is my OSHUN and always will be. Her big beautiful brown eyes were like ponds of peace and pure bliss. Her lips soft as a baby's skin and as gentle as a mother's touch. Knowing where her dream would take her, I paid what I felt was the ultimate price. Letting go of the better part of me.

We knew each other so well we could finish each other's sentence. Like a fine piano we were in tuned with one another. Inseparable is what most had to say yet look at us now. The love I have for her will never undercut the love for the one I'm destined to be with. Trust I have enough love to go around but I am only willing to allow that special someone the right to bare and embrace all that I have. Getting back to my beautiful Black and Latin love I must say she is all I need or ever dreamed of. The fact that she and I are able to be friends just adds that extra bonus to our relationship. It's hard to find the best of both worlds but I must admit I did and I let it go. I was told if a love is true let it go and it will come back to you. Sometimes you have to let the bird fly free and not try to cage it.

"No Regrets"

Table of Contents

"No Regrets"

Chapter 1
The day my life changed

It was a warm spring day in April I will never forget. The air was crisp and fresh, feeling the warm sunrays on my skin, birds chirping and kids playing outside. Some playing double-dutch others playing curb ball. This day would change my life forever when an angel named Sabrina moved into our neighborhood. Her long thick curly black hair had all the little boys on the block gazing at her. Kids walking up to her trying to find out who she was. I was a mature ten year old when she first walked up to my driveway where I was sitting waiting for my turn to play double-dutch.

Hi my name is Sabrina. And what's your name?
She asked.
My name is Asia.
Do you mind if I sit with you Asia?
No, I don't mind you can have a seat.
So, Sabrina what brings you to the
neighborhood? I asked her.
Well, my mom and dad divorced and we had to
find another place to live. So, we came to live
with my grandmother until my mom can figure
things out.
That's cool I live with my grandmother as well
but my mom still lives with my dad. They
wanted me to attend a better school so that's
why I'm living here.
Asia, can I ask why are you just sitting in the
drive way?
Well, if you must, I was waiting for my turn
to jump double-dutch but I no longer want to
any more.
Is there something you would like to do?
No! Sabrina said in her angelic voice.
So how old are you, Sabrina?
I'm eleven and you are?
I am ten, I replied.
So, Asia what is it that you like doing for fun?

Besides playing double-dutch I love to draw, read and go skating. What about you Sabrina? I love to go skating as well she replied. Maybe one day we can go.

Sure.

Sabrina how about today if you want to?

Sabrina looked at me smiled and replied I would like to. Just let me run next door and ask my mom if it is ok.

Ok. Well, I'm going to do the same and we will meet back here.

Sure, she replied. She began to get up to go ask her mother if she could go.

Oh, how my heart began to beat like African drums at the thought of us together skating. Then I realized that I was crushing on her already. In the back of my mind, I was praying that I didn't do anything to scare her away. I knew I liked girls but I did not know how I was going to tell her or if I even wanted to. Hell, I just met her and only knew her for like a second. As I was coming out of the house, she had just reached the bottom of the driveway with her skates.

Sabrina before we go skating, I want you to meet my grandmother so she will be comfortable letting me hang with you and maybe I can meet your mother as well.

Sure, why not I believe we are going to be best friends anyway.

We turned to walk to my front door, grandma I yelled as she came to the door. Yes, Asia she answers.

Grandma I wanted you to meet Sabrina she's the one I'm going skating with.

Well, hello young lady, how are you? My grandmother asked as she extended her hand to shake Sabrina's hand.

I'm fine nice to meet you, Sabrina said with a smile.

As you already know I'm Asia's grandmother Mrs. Johnson but everyone calls me grandma.

Nice to meet you grandma.

My grandmother gave her a warm smile.

I leaned in to give my grandmother a kiss on her cheek, then we headed to her place so that I could meet her mother.

Mami, Mami she yelled through the door. Her mother came to the door.

Mami, I want you to meet my new friend Asia we are going skating together.

Hola Asia, nice to meet you I'm Mrs. Sanchez.

Nice to meet you Mrs. Sanchez.
As I shook her hand, she gave me one of the sincerest smiles.
We are going skating now, I will see you in a little while.
You two have fun and be careful.
We will we both yelled back as we skated away. It was an instant friendship between the two of us as if we grew up together. We laughed, skated, talked and just had a good time when Sabrina skates rolled over a few pebbles and she fell. I rushed over to see if she was ok. She had just scraped her knee nothing major but I knew then it was time to head home. As I helped her up, brushed her off. Come on it's time to get you home and cleaned up.
She looked at me and smiled.
Thank you but I'm ok.
I know but I just want to be sure we can return tomorrow if you feel up to it.
She looked at me smiled at me once again and said I would like that.
It took us a while to make it back home because we actually walked back instead of trying to skate. We took our skates off and hung them around our necks walking in our sock

back home. My grandmother is going to tear my butt up for walking in my socks, I hope she understands why I did it. I could see that the pain was starting to set in as the tears welled up in her eyes but she wouldn't let them fall.

Sabrina are you ok? I asked.

Yes! Thanks for asking.

Here use this as I reached in my pocket and handed her the tissue I had in my shorts from earlier.

What is this for she asked? As she stretched her hand out for the napkin.

So, you can wipe your eyes. Its ok you can cry in front of me plus I know you have to be hurting. That was a bad fall you took.

You're right it was and it does hurt but I feel I always have to be strong.

Sabrina, you don't always have to be strong with me deal, as I opened up my arms to give her a hug.

Deal… she replied as she hugged me back.

For the first time in her life, she felt it was ok to show her emotions. All I could think about as we walked back was there was nothing I could do. I watched her as she limped from pain. Each step seemed to get worse and worse.

Constantly wiping her eyes. I just wanted to take her pain away. Over and over again I questioned my deep concerns for her. Being that I had just met her. How do I continue to have her as a friend knowing I'm starting to have feelings for her? This was a lot of pressure for a ten-year-old. The things I was experiencing were things that I should not be experiencing as a kid. Plus, this wasn't acceptable in the black community. The love I had for the same sex was a taboo and frowned upon. See regardless as to how I felt for anyone I had to always keep it hid and bottled up inside. This was just something the black communities didn't want to talk about or tolerate. Man, they will have you at the alter trying to pray the demon out of you. Those are just the facts.

I rang the doorbell for her mom to come open the door.

Mrs. Sanchez saw that Sabrina was hurt and asked what happened.

Mrs. Sanchez we were skating and her front wheels got caught up on a pebble. She fell and hurt herself. We came back as soon as it happened.

Asia, thank you for bringing her back home and making sure she was ok. Get home safe and she will see you tomorrow.

Good night Sabrina, good night Mrs. Sanchez I said as I turned to walk home. It seemed like I was walking a mile to get home. I just wanted to ease all of Sabrina's pain but there was nothing I could do. My heart broke. As I walked through the door my grandmother asked, Asia are you ok baby?

Yes ma'am, I'm ok.

You look worried baby, whatever it is it will be ok. Come give me a hug.

My grandmother always knew what to do to make me feel better. Tired so I went to take a bath and get ready for bed I have a long day at school tomorrow.

The very next day I saw Sabrina as I was walking to the bus stop.

Hey Sabrina I yelled as she was already standing at the bus stop.

Hey Asia!

How's your knee?

It's much better.

I made it in the nick of time the school bus was

just pulling up as we finished talking.
We sat together on the bus and just got to know each other. Upon our arrival at school, we found out that we had all the same classes which made it easier for her. Since she was new to the school that helped her out knowing she knew someone. Over the course of the school year, you would have thought we were sisters. When you saw one you saw the other. We did everything together. We had developed a bond like none I had ever had before with anyone other than my family.

During our school holiday's and breaks we went to each other's family house to spend time as a big family. Her mother and my grandmother became like mother and daughter. Being that my grandmother was a much older woman it made things easier knowing she has someone to help out while I was in school. Mrs. Sanchez was like a mother figure to me since my mother wasn't around much. As the years went on, she and I were inseparable. The two of us were like water and air. You wouldn't get one without the other. Then all of a sudden something happened that would shake me to my core. I have to be honest I wasn't nowhere ready for what was about to happen. How do I prepare for what was about to change my life?

No Regrets

Chapter 2
She found someone

As we entered into our second year of middle school this was the year that my life was about to change and not for the better. This young big head, little beautiful eyed, athletic, muscle bound, seventh grader decided he wanted to be Sabrina's boyfriend. I must admit he was cute and most of the little girls wanted Mr. Marcus. Even though I can't blame him she wasn't supposed to break the bond between us. Sabrina and Marcus began to hang out more and more as they got to know each other. It was always done in secret. Mrs. Sanchez didn't play about having boys coming around to hang out with the little girls from the neighborhood. So, in order to make sure she was happy I went along with what they started. The agony of seeing them together, hugging, playing, laughing and having fun made my heart cringe. I can't be mad though; all she knew was I wanted her as my friend nothing more. I didn't have the courage to tell her my truth of how I felt about her. Especially since I knew she wasn't into girls like I was. I felt she would be mine when the time is right. Even though I wanted her right then I knew the timing was off. I couldn't help but feel like she was waking up every morning thinking of the wrong person when in fact she should be thinking about me. Sabrina would either call me on the phone or come to the house to tell me all about her and Marcus during the times they spent apart. She was my friend so of course I would sit there I heard her but I was never listening. I could have cared less about what her and that damn boy was doing. One day after school Sabrina asked me if I would try out for the volley ball team with her. I said yes knowing I wanted to play basketball. We went to try outs in the gym it was so many girls who wanted to make the team. A few days went by they posted the roster and of course we made the team. She and I

joined the varsity volleyball team. I knew there
had to be a catch and what do you know, it was
so she could spend more time with Marcus. He
tried out for basketball, football, soccer,
baseball, and track. Needless to say, I wasn't
surprised that he was able make all the teams.
Now this was another thing I had to sit around
and watch her cheer for him when we were not
playing. Truth be told I don't even like
volleyball even though I'm good at it. I had to
find a way for us to have some time to
ourselves without her little friend around. I was
able to watch her in those little shorts running
up and down the court. It was so hard for me to
focus and not let anyone know what it was I
was looking at. One afternoon while we were
still in practice who did I see walk into the gym
and sit down. Yes, Mr. Marcus and his goon
squad. I promise you he is like a bad rash that
just won't go away. When you think it's gone,
here he comes reappearing? Why can't he just
give her some space or is it that he can sense
how I feel about Sabrina? After practice him
and his big-headed best friend Miguel walked
us home. Sabrina and Marcus walked hand in
hand and I was left to fight this knuckle head

off of me. He was cute with some beautiful eyes and curly hair but I knew who and what I wanted. I could use this to my advantage to always be around no matter what as long as Miguel didn't try me. I believe this could work. Or so I thought right up until he tried to kiss me as we reached our street. I had to punch him in his chest to get him off of me all the while Marcus and Sabrina were lip locked. This went on day after day Monday through Friday. Also, when we could sneak away on the weekends and after every game we played or he played. This cycle only seemed to get worse for me. They came around so much that when my grandmother and Mrs. Sanchez saw them, they both thought they were from our neighborhood. Neither one of them had a problem then with us hanging out. Our parents felt some kind of relief knowing we have male friends who would look out for us if something was to happen. It got so bad that they came over for family dinners. Their parents got to know our parents and then we all went on family vacations together. We even attended the same church together. I never saw this taking place. I kept thinking, how did I let it get this far. Here I am caught up and out of luck. Yes, I am happy for them but he has what's mine and I'm not happy about it. God has some serious explaining to do. Throughout middle school and high school, it was always us four Sabrina, Marcus, Miguel and myself. How did this happen to me? I promise you we were together so much Miguel believed he was my boyfriend. We are great friends to each other there is no question about that. There was nothing that he and I wouldn't do for each other but it couldn't be anything more than that. How did my pain become my reality? How can I turn this situation around and not hurt anyone in the process? I ask myself over and over again do I want to be the cause of Sabrina's heartbreak. Do I sacrifice my feelings and hurt or do I come clean and possibly lose my best friend? This has got to be the worst thing ever. This was too much to bear and I didn't see it changing any time soon. How can I continue to watch this take place? I need to do something but I have no idea of what I can do. Despite the fact that they are so happy together I hate to see it. It's a sad place to be stuck in the friend zone.

No Regrets

Chapter 3
It is what it is

How do I come to grips with all that has happened? It's been a while since I've spoken with Sabrina, she and I use to talk every day. Here it is our senior year in high school and the two of them have gotten engaged and plan to wed soon once they get settled in at school and in NY. Both plan on attending college in New York since Marcus had an uncle who passed away recently and left him a house. Marcus was his favorite nephew. I mean that's good for them but what about me. I'm starting to feel like I'm losing all that I have. What is really going on? My heart has never been this heavy and I'm feeling like I'm losing my way. My life is being turned upside down. What is my next move? Do I try and apply for the same college in NY? Do I learn to accept the pain and believe that God will work this out?

There are so many questions running through my head right now and I don't know how to make them stop. My mind has become a battlefield. My emotions are starting to get the best of me. I have to release some of these emotions quick. Before I lose it. So, I decided to go to my grandmother and talk to her about what was going on.

Grandma I need to speak with you but please tell me you won't get mad.

Asia baby what's wrong?

Grandma please don't get mad at what I'm about to say but you know Sabrina.

Baby what about Sabrina is she ok?

My grandmother asked as her voice cracked with concern.

Yes, grandma she's ok its nothing like that.

Then what is it? Grandma replied.

I've been in love with Sabrina since I first met her and now, she will be leaving to go to New York with Marcus and marry him after graduation.

My grandmother chuckled and grinned placed
her hand on my face and said:
Aww baby I knew you loved her I saw it in
your eyes. The way you looked at her when you
two were together told it all. You know you
can't hide anything from me anyway. I know
my baby and I know your heart. It's
understandable for you to feel the way you do.
Asia baby, you can either allow her to see if
this is what she truly wants with Marcus or tell
her how you feel. There are
no other options. Asia if you truly love her
at some point you will have to let her know.
Love Sabrina enough to see her be happy and if
at any point in her life she begins to miss you
she will find her way back to you.
I hung my head and sighed. Grandma how do I
begin to lover her enough to let her go?
Asia you already know the answer to that.
Yes, I do but I was hoping that you would say
something different.
Baby you know grandma loves you and only
wants to see you happy but this is something
you have to figure out on your own. Love isn't
always easy but it is always worth it.
As she wiped the tears away from my eyes.

Grandma I love you.

I love you too baby.

At that moment my grandmother opened her arms so that I could lay my head on her chest. Anytime I was troubled my grandmother's chest was always a place I

could lay my head to find peace and solace. As the tears continued to flow from my eyes I laid there in silence. Far too long have I allowed my love for Sabrina to live in the bruising darkness which caused more pain to me than anything else in life. My heart was under siege as I laid face down in confusion. Do I tell her how I feel or do I continue to be there for my friend?

My heart struggles for peace and harmony as I sit marinating in gloom. I was at war with myself. The moment of truth was forcefully approaching as I know I have to be honest with her and myself. There is an undying yearning to tell Sabrina how I feel but a greater desire to see her happy. I have to be honest and let the chips fall where they may. Later that day I decided to walk over to Sabrina's house so I can have a minute to sit and talk with her. Before her and Marcus hooked up, she would come to me but I guess it is what it is now. It was a gloomy day which made things even worst. I felt like this was a sign to walk away. My chest was heavy as a ships anchor. My head pounding as if I was being hit with ten thousand fists upon my head. I approached the front door; I heard a still soft voice say; hey Asia I was just thinking about you.

It was Sabrina as she opened the screen door for me to come in.

Good afternoon Mrs. Sanchez, how are you?

I'm fine Asia how are you my dear?

I'm good, I replied.

That's good well you two go on upstairs so you can catch up.

Yes, ma'am we both said at the same time.

If you need me, I will be over to your house Asia.

Ok, grandma will love to see.

See you girls later.

Asia what's wrong? You seem sad.

I'm okay, just been doing a lot of thinking and I'm starting to miss my friend.

What do you mean?

Well once we graduate Sabrina, you're moving and I won't be able to see you as much.

I know, I feel the same way Asia but I promise to keep in touch.

Sabrina, can I tell you something and promise not to get mad.

What is it? You know you can tell me anything.

Well, you know that I love you and you mean the world to me.

Yes, I know that. Now why would I get mad over that?

Wait…There's more… I replied.

I don't just love you I am also in love with you and have been since I met you. I was afraid to tell you because I never wanted to lose my friend or my friendship with you. So, I have held it in for quite some time now.

Sabrina sat there with a blank expression on her face, one I couldn't read and I had never seen before. Silence filled the room so many thoughts began to run through my mind I just wanted to go hide but I was frozen.

Asia I've known for some time that your feelings for me were stronger than what you could admit to but you know I'm engaged to Marcus. I love you and always will, this is the

only love I can give you and trust me I have never taken how you feel for me for granted. You will always be my best friend; I will always love you and pray you will always love me.
Loving you is something I will always do Sabrina. You never have to worry about that. Asia, I love you never forget that.
I won't.
As she leaned in and gave me a hug my heart cried out like rocks of old times. The one thing I've always wanted was the one thing that caused my soul to ache. Feeling as if my heart was just sentenced to the fiery pits of hell. Burning like lava against concrete.
We looked at each other and smiled then embraced each other once again. It hit me; this was the moment my grandmother was talking about I had no other choice but to love her enough to see her be happy.
We sat, talked and laughed in a way we hadn't done in a very long time. Although the debris of what I once hoped for flooded my chest I began to turn my face towards finding my peace. Letting the songs of our laughter

ease my roaring seas. It was getting late so I got up to leave Sabrina gave me a hug like that she had never given me before. It seemed more intimate and innocent. To my surprise our eyes locked and before I knew it, I kissed her she didn't push me away but softly kissed me back. I kissed her lightly on her forehead before I left to go home. I knew she was not leaving Marcus. I know she will always love me and continue to be my best friend. Thinking back on the

moment as I walked home, I felt better about telling Sabrina how I was feeling and was able to move past my feelings for her. I open the door and was greeted with the warmest smiles from two amazing women I loved so much. Asia baby won't you come and sit with us for a minute.

I sat down at the dinner table with my grandmother and Mrs. Sanchez. My grandmother looked at me and said we were just talking about you and Sabrina.

Oh really! So, what were you two talking about?

Well Asia I was telling grandma about Sabrina and how she was having a hard time lately.

What do you mean having a hard time?
She came to me the other day confused
about her direction in life and wasn't sure
which way to go.
She finally admitted to me that she loved
you but she wanted to marry Marcus and
didn't know how to tell you.
I just sat there stunned, speechless, and
numb with a blank gaze on my face.
So that's when grandma was telling me how
you felt about Sabrina. So, once I saw the hurt
on your face, I figured that you were going
through the same thing as she was. I left the
house so that you two could talk I saw that
there was a lot that you both need to talk about.
Neither one of us want either one of you to hurt
or be unhappy.
Asia baby, how did it go? My grandmother
asked.
You were right grandma I told her how I felt
and she told me how she felt. Then I kissed her
and realized at that instant I had to love her
enough to let her go and be happy. I have to
admit I will always love her and wait for her
because I can't give my heart to
anyone the way I gave my heart to her.

We will keep in touch and remain best friends and whatever is meant to be will be. There was nothing else left for me to do. As soft siliques played melancholy melodies on the stings of my heart. I have to accept things for what they are.
It is what it is!

No Regrets

Chapter 4
Graduation

The time was at hand and just hours before graduation. Emotions are running high with excitement, happiness, joy and relief. Sabrina and I were just leaving the nail salon from getting our eyebrows waxed, our manicures and pedicures. Heading back to her house to get ready for graduation time seemed to pass with ease. Giggling and talking while helping each other get dressed seemed like the times when we first met.

Just as I was getting the urge to walk up behind her and kiss her on the neck her cell phone rang. Damn it! I yelled in my mind. Of course, it was that big head boy Marcus calling to tell her he loved her and can't wait to see her. I knew he made her happy and she trusted him with her whole heart. I had to find a way to channel my emotions so she wouldn't pick up on it.

How do I make peace with someone being with my woman? Her pillow soft kisses and warm hugs were supposed to be mine. But I have to settle for what I am given for now.

She put him on speaker so I could hear the conversation and so that she could continue to get dressed for graduation. Long and behold that damn Miguel had to get on the phone to say something to me. We were friends so I guess I could continue to be nice just as long as he didn't say anything that I didn't want to hear. Even though over the years it seemed as if he and I were a couple my focus was always on Sabrina. But the truth of it all I would have pretended to be his girlfriend if that meant I would be able to be around her more. The four of us continued to talk and laugh as we got ready for graduation. We only had a few minutes left so we hung up and grabbed our things so we could leave.

Sabrina, could you do me one last favor before we leave?

Sure, what's that Asia?

Could you give me one last kiss? And I promise to never mention to you my feelings for you no more unless you ask me to.

She looked at me and smiled and said yes it would be my pleasure. Leaning in as we met half way our lips touched and she kissed me so endearing like I was the only per she loved and it was our wedding day. She even slid in a little tongue. Never did I expect it would feel so virtuous or last as long as it did. We hugged and left for graduation. Her mom, her grandmother and my grandmother were dropping us off. We held hands the whole way there smiling and looking at each other.

Sabrina, I got you a gift for graduation here you go.

Asia, I got you something as well here you go. Thank you we both said in unison. We opened our gift we gave each other an infinity love necklace one was yellow gold and the other was white gold. It was a symbol that our love would never end but last for infinity.

We just arrived at the Arena where graduation was being held. We got out to go inside while they went to park. As soon as we entered who did we run into, yes of course Marcus and

Miguel. Me being the person I am I pretended to be happy to see them and I must admit I was a little. It was a turning point in all our lives. Marcus and Sabrina lips locked and Miguel gave me the warmest hug he made me feel special. We all went to the back so that we could get ready for the lineup. Ok everyone A-M on the left and N-X on the right let's get ready graduates. It's almost time to walk out to our seat. Mrs. Holmes was the school principal. She stood erected looked out into the class and began to speak:

I just want to take the time out to tell you all that it has been a pleasure watching all of you boys and girls grow up to be handsome young men and amazing young women. These past four years I have watched you all grow and overcome many challenges. I wish you much success in your futures and in all that you do. It has been an honor and pleasure to be your principle to help guide you into greatness. May this next chapter in your life bring great success and happiness. I love you all and I will truly miss seeing your beautiful faces.

Mrs. Holmes, we love you too. We appreciate you and we are thankful for all that you have done, said the class valedictorian. We began to applaud her as we broke out in a heartfelt cheer. A tear dropped her eye as she turned around to get
ready for the graduation. We all walked through the curtains. Walked to our seats. As the program continued on, I watched as all the wonderful faces and people walk across the stage to receive their diplomas. You can hear the cheers of the family members and friends of the graduates. We all had received our diplomas and was seated back in our chairs. Mrs. Holmes walked up to the microphone once everyone received their diplomas. Graduates please, switch your tassels from left to right. You have now officially graduated and this is a new chapter you are embarking on. Give yourselves a round of applause. All you seen was caps being thrown up in the air and
cheering constantly. My mind shifted quickly from cheer to brokenness knowing that this would be my last leg of this journey with

Sabrina. It all was coming to an end so fast.
Damn, what do I do now?

No Regrets

Chapter 5
A new chapter unfolds

High school is over and everyone has gone off to college except me. I can't do another four years of Marcus and Sabrina. Or pretending that Miguel and I are more than friends in order to be able to spend more time with Sabrina. Even though she is my heartbeat and joy I had to be able to walk away and find a way to be ok without her. Now is the time I need to focus on myself especially since college been started and I still haven't heard from Sabrina. I knew things would change but I thought I would at least hear from her once a week. Hell, maybe once a month. I began to feel as if was no longer of any importance to her. Why is it so hard to stop focusing on Sabrina and focus more on me? I have work to do and need to shake this off. While taking online classes I decided to check out different workshops so that I can better my craft. I decided to take my passion of photography and turn it into a career.

Once a month at the downtown library in one of their conference rooms they sponsor a photographer workshop every third Wednesday at 6pm. Wednesday evening I decided to attend the photographer's meet-up workshop at the library. When I ran into one of my high school classmates.

Asia Johnson, is that you?

Yes, it is…

Phylicia Love, how have you been?

I've been fine thanks for asking.

That's good, Phylicia I thought you moved away after graduation. What caused you to stick around? I asked.

No girl, I landed my dream job. The money is great, my family is here what else can I ask for. Besides the company is paying for me to get my degree.

So, Ms. Asia what have you been up to?

Well, I decided to live out my passion as a

photographer so I'm working as a freelancer while going to school.

Is that so? Phylicia replied.

Asia, do you happen to have any of your work with you.

Yes, I do as a matter of fact. Let's take a seat right here while I get them out of my bag. I reached inside my black messenger bag and pulled out my portfolio. Here you go.

Phylicia took her time browsing through the photos with a smile on her face. But I can't say if it's good or bad only time will tell.

Asia your work is amazing I think I found what I've been looking for.

What do you mean? I asked.

Well, my purpose for coming here tonight was for me to find someone who may be a great fit as our company's photographer for advertisement and company events. Here's my card give me a call tomorrow so I can schedule a meeting with you and Ms. Mya Hill. She is the founder and CEO of the marketing firm I work for. If all works out you would have landed yourself a big account.

Phylicia thank you so much this is what I was hoping for; for a while and why I decided to come tonight.

I tell you things have a way of working themselves out.

Asia it was great seeing you again, I'm going to mingle a little before I get out of here. Please make sure to give me a call.

Will do I promise. I replied.

We hugged then went about our way. Feeling great I started back networking before the workshop began. So, consumed with the conversation and opportunity that has been placed in front of me I totally zoned out. Thinking of all the possibilities that can come my way with this door opening I couldn't focus on what the speakers were teaching and telling us about tricks we can use. Once I began to focus, I noticed that the class was ending. Time to grab a bite to eat and go home. The next morning, I called Phylicia and she scheduled a meeting this Friday for eight o'clock in the morning. I didn't expect for things to go so quickly I had to prepare for this meeting. Printing out my forms and resume' just in case she asks for it. I made sure to get enough rest the night before so I can make a good impression on Ms. Hill. Eight o'clock Friday

morning came fast. I arrived at A&M
Marketing Firm fifteen minutes early. That
always looks good to a potential client. As I sat
in the lobby her secretary came out.
Ms. Johnson; Ms. Hill will see you now.
It seemed as if the hallway would never end.
We reached her office.
Ms. Hill, Ms. Johnson is here for her eight
o'clock.
Thank you, Cindy, send her in please.
I'm Mya Hill nice to meet you Ms. Johnson,
how are you?
I'm blessed thanks for asking.
How are you?
I'm blessed as well.
I have heard nothing but great things about your
work. Phylicia speaks highly of you and that
isn't something she does often.
Thank you, I replied.
Do you have some of your work with you that I
can take a look at?
Yes, ma'am I do.
I handed her my portfolio as she sat behind her
desk flipping page by page.
I can't read her face, I'm nervous.
Does she like my work?

Does she hate it?
I feel myself beginning to sweat. She reaches the last page, closes the book looks and me and says: you have a great eye Ms. Johnson. She asked me a bunch of questions throughout this interview process. Finally, the questions were over.
I can't wait to work with you Ms. Johnson, there has to be a trial run just to see if you can truly be a great fit. How about this. I need some personal photos taken, if I like the results then the job is yours. We can discuss prices at that time. Have you heard of Monae' Art Gallery?
Yes, I have.
Great meet me there at 9 am tomorrow, all you will need is your camera. I will see you then. See you tomorrow.
We stood up, gave each other a hand shake and I exited the office. Walking down the hallway I saw Phylicia. I waved and said thank you.
She smiled and said you're welcome.
Morning came so quick and it was time for me to put my game face on. I was so nervous I felt like a hooker in church when I was getting

ready to take Ms. Hills photos. But as we got into the grove of things, she made me feel comfortable. I must admit she is a pleasure to work with and the camera loves her. After the photo shoot she invites me out for drinks we sat and talked. To my surprise I found out we have more in common than I thought.

Asia, what do you do for fun?

Taking photos, that's my fun. Why do you ask?

I was just wondering. You seem to be so focused and married to your passion.

To be honest Ms. Hill I am. This is all I focus on, morning, noon and night. I want to have my own business one day. So, I won't ease up until I reach my goal.

I admire that about you. Let me ask you this what do you think about art?

Nothing, I feel sometimes it's hard to interrupt what the artist is trying to say.

How about you come walk with me and I will teach you about some of my favorite pieces.

I would love that Ms. Hill.

As we walk and talk, I find myself admiring Mya more than the art. As she is talking, I am watching the curve of her lips, the way she smiles, the tone of her voice as she talks about her favorite artist. I fall back a little to get a better look at her frame. A perfect picture I might say. At the end of the tour, she asks do you like what you see?

Excuse me? What do you mean by that?

Ms. Johnson did you think you could check me out without me noticing?

I thought I could, I apologize if I made you feel uncomfortable. But I won't apologize for looking.

She smiles. Asia, I checked you out when you first came to my office so I guess we are even. We laughed and continued our conversation.

So now that I have shown you my favorite artist, how about dinner at my place tonight? No pressure I would like to get to know you better. It's ok if you would like to decline.

I hesitated but she is looking so damn good I thought no but Yes came out of my mouth.

Great I will text you my address, see you later. See you later.

We embrace each other much longer than normal then she kisses me. With me being so weak for a beautiful black woman I kiss her back.

I must admit the attention feels good. Hell,

there is no harm in having a little dinner. Plus, what's the worst thing that could happen? I got the feeling that there might be more than dinner going on. Tonight, is going to be an interesting night. Can't wait to see what unfolds. My lawd help me and have mercy on me. I don't know what I am getting into but I know I am anxious to find out. Plus, I have a thing for slightly older women.

No Regrets

Chapter 6
Dinner and Wine

I kept thinking to myself what I am getting myself into. I know I have always been attracted to women but I only wanted to be with one and that's Sabrina. But I know at some point I have to accept the fact that chapter may be closed. While sitting in my thoughts I couldn't help but to wonder how tonight will turn out. I left the museum earlier feeling wonderful and beautiful to have caught the eye of a gorgeous woman. I can't believe I am about to open up and allow someone the possibility to come in to my life. I can't just sit around and wait for Sabrina I have to go on with my life as well. This will be a great start if

I can only figure out what I am wearing tonight. Destroying my closet and bedroom trying to find something to wear. I didn't want to overdress or underdress my nerves started to get the best of me. Beep, beep... a text came through. Looking at my phone it was Ms. Hill. The text read:

Looking forward to seeing you tonight and getting to know you better. My address is 824 Myra Drive. See you soon.

Smiling like I had just received my first, if you will go out with me yes or no letter. I giggled. I'm tripping. Time was winding down I jumped in the shower right quick. Put on a pair of jeans pressed of course and a nice blouse, boots so that I would feel comfortable even though I felt like a bunch of banshees were running wild on the inside. Jumped in the car typed the address in the GPS and headed to her house. As I'm driving to Mya's place, I reached in the glove box to grab my gum, have to make sure my breath is on point. I text her while stopped at the red light to let her know I should be there in about five minutes.

She responded see you then. I pulled up in the drive way, looked in the mirror to make sure I didn't have anything in my nose or between my teeth and then I got out. Rang the doorbell. Mya opened the door with a glass of wine.

Hello Asia, I'm glad that you decided to have dinner with me tonight. Come in she said as she was handed me the glass of wine. Please leave your shoes at the front door. I just had my floors refinished so please forgive me.

That's not a problem I replied.

As I walked in, I was amazed, to how huge her house was. Tranquil aromas of lavender filled the air. Warm, peaceful and hominess cascaded throughout her place. Her home was exquisite, she had so many paintings on her walls from some of the most influential artist. A great eye for worth and splendor in more than just art. Make yourself at home she yelled from the kitchen. Wow, you really do like art I yelled back. She exits the kitchen to place dinner on the table. I look at her she smiles and said yes. I do love the finer things in life. I'm all about the quality and value of a thing. Maybe some time we can visit different art galleries to purchase some paintings for your home if that's something you're interested in.

Sure, I would love that, I smiled back. Please come, sit dinner is now ready and we can eat. I'm here to serve you tonight. I hope you brought your appetite with you?

Yes, Ms. Hill I did. Let's see how well you throw down in the kitchen.

We laughed and looked at each other. She walks over to my side of the table grabs my dish and began fixing my plate something that only my grandmother had done for me. Or I for someone else. I couldn't help but watch her every move as my eyes surveyed her body. Gazing over her hands, her arms, down her back to her plumped ass. I tell you baby was stacked very well. Her demeanor held me captive. As her words faded into the background. Asia, Asia…Mya called my name.

Excuse me I'm sorry what did you say?

I asked if this was enough?

That is plenty, thank you.

She sat my plate down back in front of me and began to fix her dinner.

She sat down across from me and asked.

Ms. Asia would you like to say grace?

Yes, as she held her hands out for mine. We

held hands bowed our heads and I began to bless the food.

Father thank you for this meal we are about to partake in, I ask that you bless it and bless the hands that prepared it. May it be nourishing to our bodies in your holy name we pray Amen. Amen she replied.

Mya, tell me a little more about yourself, where are you from, how was it growing up? Etc., etc. Ok, well I am from Jacksonville, Florida born and raised, I'm the oldest of two girls, my mother and father are still married till this day and still live in the same home I grew up in. My mother is a retired school teacher. My father is a retired marine. My family is extremely close they have been so supportive of my alternative lifestyle, I am so grateful for that. Umm let's see what else. I'm a Virgo born August 24th I love art of course; I love hiking and to read. What about yourself Ms. Asia? I too am from Jacksonville, Florida born and raised. I'm the only child my parents moved to

North Carolina when I was young. My grandmother is a retired nurse she raised me and she has supported me in everything I do. As far as my lifestyle she supports it but to be honest I haven't had many experiences. I have only wanted one woman but I don't think that will happen.

Why do you say that, Asia?

Well, it's my best friend but she is engaged to her high school boyfriend and they live in New York. But that is water under the bridge.

Asia, can I ask you a personal question?

Sure.

Have you ever been with a woman?

Almost choking I replied. No. I have not.

I have never thought of being with someone other than her.

So, do you think you will be open to giving someone else a chance?

Yes, of course if she is worth it.

Mya smiling and replied great, I'm glad to hear that you are open.

We sat and talked as we finished our dinner.

Asia would you like some more?

No, thank you. That was enough and I have to say you know your way around the kitchen.

Why thank you, I'm glad you approved. Go
over to the couch while I clear the table.
No, Mya let me help you that's the least I can
do.
Asia that is so sweet of you, thank you.
I grabbed the plates and she grabbed the
glasses. She put the glasses in the dishwasher,
just as I was about to put the dishes in the
dishwasher she turned around and we locked
eyes. We gazed at each other for a few seconds.
I then gained my composure and put the dishes
in the dishwasher then walked over to the
couch. I couldn't believe that I was looking at
another woman with interest. I couldn't resist
she was beautiful, stunning, smart, intelligent
and fine as hell. I would be a fool not to at least
try things out if presented. She brought with her
two glasses and a bottle of wine. She set on the
couch looked and me and said I was hoping we
could watch a movie together. Unless you are
ready to leave?
No, I'm enjoying myself and a movie will be
fine.
She fills a glass with wine then hands it to me
then turned poured her a glass. She turned on
the tv., then the DVD player and hit play.

What movie is it?

Soulmates undone.

What is this movie about?

It is about two females one is a dancer who's a lesbian and a writer who is confused about what she wants. Where two souls are destined to find each other, I believe they call it "twin flame". I thought this would

be a perfect movie to watch.

Cool, it sounds interesting.

She picked up her glass of wine and came close to me, I wrapped my arm around her as we snuggled to watch the movie. She grabbed her throw and covered us with it. The movie was almost over, I felt my pulse rise and I began to feel myself getting heated. I think I have had one glass too many. I leaned forward to place my glass in the table as I sat back, I kissed her on the forehead. She gently caressed my face. I reached over and took her glass out of her hand placed in on the table. I looked her in the eye leaned forward seductively as she looked me in my eyes and kissed her. Her lips were so soft, warm and gentle. She then wrapped her arms around my waist laying me on my back. Slowly she began to unbutton my shirt, while caressing my chest she then unbuttons her shirt pressing her body against mine. She then unbuttons my pants slowly taking them off as I began to do the same with her. We look at each other as we lay on the couch unclothed. She kisses every inch of my body, straddles across my lap while kissing me. She then places her hand between my legs. I feel myself getting wet as she eases her way down between my legs. Kissing my inner thigh down to my toes. She takes my left leg placing it on her back. Places her head right above my womb of life sliding my panties to the side she kisses then licks my clit. I can feel her warm, thick, long tongue going up and down, in and out of my gold mine. She sucks my clit, sticks her fingers inside of me. I start to moan; she penetrates me with her fingers faster and faster yet gentle and slow. My back arches the sensation becomes intense. I grab a pillow off the couch place it over my mouth to muffle my moans. In that final moment I yell out a sigh of pure passion as I explode. She comes back up to kiss me. She runs her hands over my breast then holds me. I kiss her so endearingly then I held her as she lies on my chest. That

experience was something so pleasing and pure. But to my surprise it wouldn't end there. As she stood up took my hand and led me to her bedroom. Little did I know she had this planned out and I was in for a big surprise tonight. Lit candles and roses lined the hallway leading to her bedroom. Soft music playing in the background. Body oils and a variety of toys stretch across her dresser. She gently laid me on my back. Running her fingers over my skin and she made my body quiver with unadulterated desire and passion. As the flicker from the flame of the candles showed a lovely silhouette of her beautiful frame. As our bodies press poetically against each other. Caressing each other we kissed as if it was for the very first time. Fervently, as our fingers intertwined in moments of ecstasy and bliss. Did I forget to mention baby was good and seasoned if you know what I mean. I was in for a great night and willing to enjoy every second of it. The night was
just beginning. And the pleasure had already begun.

No Regrets

Chapter 7
Another year passed

It has been two years now since Sabrina and Marcus moved to New York to attend college along with Miguel. I began to feel so neglected. No matter how much time I was spending with another woman I still missed my friend.
Working as a freelance has had many perks and some challenges. Thankfully it has allowed me to meet many amazing people. I have been working hard so I can start my own business. Once I'm
finish with my last course. My goal is to apply for a business loan soon after I am finished with all my classes. If I work hard enough, I may be able to fund my own business. Owning it out

right. Even though I have been missing Sabrina, spending time with Mya has been a pleasure. Mya is a very beautiful, intelligent and a mouth-watering delight. Often keeping me occupied and showing me things, I never thought I would experience. Art shows, fancy dinners, vacations and amazing sex Mya had me thinking about a relationship. Could I truly give Mya my all? Or will I keep hoping Sabrina comes back to me. Since she and I never discussed being in a relationship I figured we would just enjoy every minute. Taking nothing for granted. It was late one Friday night I was looking over some proofs from a photoshoot I had that morning. I received a call from Sabrina.

Hello, my friend it has been a while, how are you Ms. Sabrina?

I'm ok Sabrina replied.

Asia how have you been?

Honestly, I've been busy but ok and missing you. I wish you were here.

Me too…

So, my lovely Sabrina what has been going on with you.

Not much just school and getting used to being away from my family. But most of all I just wanted to talk to my friend. By the way Marcus and I have set a date for our wedding and I need you to be there for me.

You know I will be Sabrina regardless as long as you are happy that's all that matters to me.

Thank you, Asia that means a lot. I will be coming home in a few weeks to go dress shopping with my mom. I was hoping you would be able to join us.

Of course, any chance I can get to see my friend I am going to take it.

So, Sabrina how has living in New York been? How is Miguel? I haven't heard from him since you all left for college.

It is different from high school and Florida but I'm slowly adjusting. It's a faster pace up here. Miguel is ok he's in overload from all the females here on campus. Since you didn't ask about Marcus he is doing well.

So, you picked up on that, I'm sorry I can't help it Sabrina my feelings haven't changed. But I promise I will try to do better.

Thank you, Sabrina replied.

I heard that grandma and mom have been spending a lot of time together since we graduated.

Yes, grandma and your mom have gotten close its like we are becoming a tight nit family.

That's good I really miss you all. That is why I am having my wedding back home.

That's great I replied. I know your mom is ecstatic about that.

Yes, she is Sabrina replied.

How does Marcus feel about that?

He is happy with whatever I decide as long as I marry him.

I giggle just a little.

What's funny? Sabrina asked.

Nothing is funny I was just picturing him nodding and agreeing to whatever it is you want that's all. But for real, will you let me know when you arrive so I can pick you up from the airport?

Yes, I will.

Ok cool.

So, Asia what have you been up to?

Well, I have been working as a freelance photographer and taking online classes so I can start my own business.

That is amazing, I'm so proud of you Asia.
Thank you that means a lot to me.
Asia, are you dating anyone right now?
Yes, I am by the way.
Who is it?
Leica, I replied.
Who is Leica? Sabrina asked.
Leica is my camera I'm dating my dream
right now.
Girl you play too much, damn Asia.
I started laughing.
That's not funny Asia I was about to hang up
on you.
Sabrina, you can't be serious right now?
Did you really think I would be dating anyone
knowing I'm waiting for you to come back to
me? Besides how can you even feel some kind
of way when you are planning a wedding or did
you forget that part?
No Asia I didn't. But I can't imagine you
giving your love to anyone else other than me.
Sabrina listen to me and listen well. My love
is for you and you only but I won't wait
forever. And to be honest you shouldn't want
me too. If I do find someone you should be
happy for me the same way I am for you. The

ball has always been in your court but you keep throwing it back to me. Don't expect me to rule out a possibility for a hope and a prayer.

Asia, I agree. You have been open and honest about how you feel about me. I know my situation and I can't help being a little selfish when it comes to you. If you do decide to date Asia, I will try my best to be happy for you.

Thank you, I appreciate your honesty and I can't ask for anything more than that. I can't wait for you to come home.

Me either she replied.

I don't know if I should tell her what has truly been going on. If she only knew what and who I had been into she would really be upset. So, I decided to leave that conversation right there. If you know what I mean. I don't need any unnecessary drama. Plus, things haven't gotten too serious

between Mya and myself. Or has it?

No Regrets

Chapter 8
The arrival

It was a late foggy Friday night about 10:30 when I got a call from an unknown number. Hesitant but I decided to answer anyway.
Hello.
Asia.
Yes, who is this?
It's me.
Me who?
Sabrina.
Girl where are you and who's phone are you calling me from?

My phone died and I forgot my charger so I am using this nice old lady's phone. I'm at the airport. Can you please come and get me? Yeah, give me about twenty minutes and I will be there. I rushed to get dressed I was so excited to see Sabrina. Doing one hundred on ninety-five smiling all the way to the airport. Twenty minutes turned into more like ten minutes. My heart was racing as if I had been running a marathon. Not knowing what to expect I put on some Sade to calm my nerves. As I approached the pickup area, I saw her standing there looking so beautiful. My heart fluttered with so many emotions. I pulled up and rolled down the window. Hey beautiful lady you need a ride?

She smiled and said yes. She put her bags in the back, got in the car and gave me a hug.

I missed you friend.

I missed you to Sabrina.

Asia, can we go to your house I don't want to wake up my mom if that's ok with you.

Sure, not a problem I replied.

It would be my pleasure to have my first overnight guest be my best friend. But I have to

let you know I only have one bed in the house
since it's just me.

That's fine it will be like the old days when we
had sleepovers. Sabrina replied.

How has grandma been doing?

She is fine as a matter of fact my house isn't
too far from her house or your moms.

That's good. I can't wait to catch up.

We talked for like what seemed forever. Before
I knew it, we made it back to my place. Ok, we
are here let me grab the bags for you.

Thank you, she replied.

I opened the front door, flipped the
switch to turn on the lights. As we both
walked in, I can see Sabrina looking around
in shock. Sabrina is everything ok?

Yes, I didn't expect your house to look like
this.

What do you mean ma'am?

I never knew you liked art. It's nice.

I'm just getting started I still have a long way to
go. But I think it fits my style.

It does, she replied. How is it I didn't know you
were so into art like this.

To be honest I wasn't at first but when you left,
I had to find something to do with my time. I

met a young lady who introduced me to art and from there the rest is history.

A young lady? Sabrina said with discontent.

Yes, a young lady, she is a client of mine and the photos I happen to take of her was at her art gallery.

Are you jealous? I asked.

No, why would I be?

I'm just asking because you seem a little rattled.

I'm not rattled and can we please change the subject.

Whatever you want my dear. Let me get you a towel and washcloth so that you can take a shower before we go to bed for the night.

Thank you, friend.

You're welcome my little jealous friend.

I'm not jealous for your information.

I giggled and put everything in the bathroom. As I lie on the bed, I hear the water of the shower hitting up against the tiles. All I can think of is going in there and making love to Sabrina in the shower. I don't know why I can't control my thoughts when I'm around her. I lose myself in her presence. As I sit on the bed my thoughts were interrupted by my name

being called.
Asia.
Yes.
Can you come here please?
I open the bathroom door enough to poke
my head in. Are you ok Sabrina?
Yes and no.
What do you need?
Can you wash my back for me?
Are you serious? You called me in here for that.
Yes. What's wrong with that Asia?
You kidding right? Do you not know how I feel
about you and you want me to wash your back?
Why are you teasing me? Can't you wash your
own back?
I'm not teasing you; I just like to have my
backed washed that's all.
Fine give me the rag big head.
She hands me the rag and all I can see is the
water running down her back into the crack of
her ass. The curves of her body and booty has
my heart beating rapidly. As the washcloth
makes love to her skin. I gently allowed the rag
to ease down the back
of her legs. Soft and slow I wash every inch of
her from the back. As I am handing her back

her washcloth, she turns around to face me. Our eyes lock as I began to look her body up and down. Slowly not to miss one inch. I look back into her eyes.

Asia come in here with me.

She takes me by my hand pulls into the shower fully dressed and all. As I'm getting in the shower, she pulls my shirt over my head undressing me. She then gets down on her knees pulling down my shorts throwing my clothes out the shower onto the floor. Aggressively pushes my back to the back of the shower wall she kisses me as if this is her last night of freedom. I kiss her back, as I now push her directly under the showerhead. Watching as the water runs over every inch of her body. I gently kiss her lips, running my tongue over her lips, down her neck as I began to kiss her breast, lick her nipples. Caressing each other I turn her around and just hold her in my arms. Pressing my body against hers I pull her hair to the side kiss the back of her neck she moans at that moment I was ready to go all in. I graciously push her back against the shower wall, placing her hands above her head intertwining our fingers we kiss with more vigor and passion than ever before. Lost in the moment we become one, the same moan, the same breath, the same movement. The pleasure intensifies I start to caress her breast as I take my right hand placing my fingers in the middle of her thighs. She wraps her leg around my waist. Each moment the heat rises and rises I gently rub her pond of pleasure placing my middle finger in her penetrating and pleasing. Her moans become louder and stronger until she climaxes and she lays her head on my chest. Relaxing her legs, she stands up she kisses me and smile. I smile back as we become immersed in each other and exit the shower. Dried each other off standing there naked hugging and holding each other as time stood still. I walked her over to the bed. I lotion the back of her neck, eased down to her back, then her legs and feet. Turned her over, lotion her neck, chest, left beast, right breast, stomach, left leg, right leg only to place my fingers inside of her one more time just to hear her moan. Turning her over I kiss her back, my tongue slides down to her ass, I kiss both of her butt checks, cuff her butt then turn her over and slid my warm tongue in and out of her. Up and down. I licked and sucked until she could no longer control herself. The need for our pj's just became a thing of the past. Her skin felt soft as velvet, her body became my canvas as I wrote sonnets and haikus, rhyme and free verse all over her body into the wee hours of the night. My tongue was the pen of a ready writer. Once the rounds came to an end. I held her close and tight as we slept afraid to let her go. I counted all my blessing that night and in the back of my mind I didn't want this night to end. I prayed that I could have moments like this with her for the rest of my life. How do you let your soulmate go and be with someone else? When you know without a shadow of a doubt, they should be with you. But what else can you do when all that matters to you is their happiness.

No Regrets

Chapter 9
Dress shopping

The next morning as I awake, I kiss Sabrina on the forehead and get up to make breakfast. I go in the bathroom brush my teeth and wash my face. I look at myself in the mirror and wonder why I don't feel bad for what just happed last night. I walk to the kitchen pull out the frying pan place it on the stove. Walk over to the fridge for some eggs, spinach, tomatoes, onions and mushrooms. I spray the pan with cooking spray, crack open several eggs and began cooking us some omelets. Once that is finished, I grab some fruit out the fridge to go with our omelet and orange juice. Placing everything on a tray I walk back into the bedroom.

Good morning sleepy head. Time to get up, I cooked us some breakfast before we head over to your mom's house.

Slowly rolling over Sabrina sits up in bed smiles.

And says good morning. Let me brush my teeth and wash my face so we can eat.

Sure, I replied.

Why didn't you wake me I could have helped you?

I didn't want to disturb you; you were sleeping so peacefully. Plus, I have that southern hospitality thang going on.

Asia you are something else.

She came back over to the bed so that we can eat together.

Thank you so much for this it means a lot to me.

You're welcome, anything for you. Sabrina, can I ask you something.

Sure, what's on your mind.

Do you regret anything about last night?

No, I was hoping that you wouldn't reject me.

Can I tell you something Asia?

Yes.

You are the first person to every make me feel completely comfortable where I was able to let go. And I had my first orgasm.

I almost choked on my orange juice.

Excuse me …

Marcus and I haven't had sex and I couldn't until I knew what it was like to feel true desire, love and passion. To be honest I don't know if I would be able to without thinking about you and wanting you.

Marcus is a good man and he makes me feel special. But I'm torn because I'm in love with you but I love him and he makes me happy.

Sabrina what was last night? Was it true or was it just so you can feel better about the decisions you are making?

Asia, last night was pure, real, undefined and unconditional. It was what I wanted but more importantly what we needed.

Well, I guess you are right. Wait are you planning on telling Marcus about what happened.

No, I don't plan on it.

Why, do you think I should tell him?

That is not my call to make. You will have to figure that out on your own. But until then let's get dressed you have a dress to pick out. We got up to get dressed, I took the tray to the kitchen put the dishes in the dishwasher. I walked back to the room Sabrina was getting out of the shower and getting dressed already. I jumped in the shower then I threw something on right quick and headed out the door got in the car. Sabrina places both her hands on my face kiss me then sits back and put her seatbelt on. I put my seatbelt on looked over at Sabrina and smiled as I pulled off. As we head to her mom's house I have so many thoughts going on in my head and emotions bubbling over in my heart. I pull up in Mrs. Sanchez's driveway. We get out the car and walk up to the door. Her mom runs out the house and hugs Sabrina like she hasn't seen her in years then comes over to me and give me a hug.

How are my girls doing? Mrs. Sanchez asked.
We are fine we replied.
Baby when did you get in.
I arrived last night ma-mi and I didn't want to wake you up so I stayed with Asia.
Oh really!!! Mrs. Sanchez said with a smile.

Sabrina asks, Mami why are you smiling so?
I am just happy to see my baby that's all.
Come on let's go pick up grandma so we
can go and pick out a wedding dress.
We headed to the bridal shop after picking my
grandma up. Even though I am happy to be
spending time with Sabrina I can't help but to
have mixed feelings about today. How can she
so easily give a piece of herself to me last night
and today pick out a wedding dress to marry
Marcus. Engulfed in my thoughts we arrive at
the bridal shop. I lingered behind everyone as
we walked into the bridal shop. Floral scents
penetrated the air while glasses of champagne
were served to customers who wanted it. Soft
deep-seated couches made it calm and relaxing.
Bright lights and beautiful gowns draped the
clothing racks. Consumed with my thoughts I
didn't even realize that Sabrina had already
gone in the back to try her dress on until I heard
the consultant's voice.
Ok ladies, here is the first dress she said as
Sabrina comes out behind her.
What do you guys think?
We all just looked and shook our heads no.
Come on let's try another dress as they turn to

walk back into the changing room.

My grandmother, grandma Sanchez and her mother discuss what they did or didn't like about the first dress. I sat there quiet not saying a word just listening.

Ok ladies, what do you think about this one as they re-enter the room.

Better her mom says but I don't think this is the one. Sabrina how do you like it? Her mom asked.

Your right ma-mi this isn't the one.

So, they exited the room again this went on and on, dress after dress and still she didn't find the one. I sat there watching as she came in the room in another dress and exited still trying to find that right dress.

Can you excuse me for a minute?

Asia where are you going baby? My grandmother asked.

No one knows Sabrina the way I do so I'm going to find her that special dress.

Ok well hurry back baby.

I walked up and down the isles until I found that dress I know I would want to marry her in. I checked the size and walked it over to the dressing room knocked on the door.

Sabrina try this one on.

She opened the door to grab the dress. I walked back to my seat sat back down with grandma Sanchez, her mother and my grandmother.

Ok ladies what do you think about this one? Sabrina came from behind the consultant stood up on the platform she was so beautiful. Her eyes lit up once she saw herself in this dress.

Mami, I think this is the one.

Everyone looked at each other and smiled. We think so too, they replied.

Sabrina looked at me and asked Asia do you like it.

Yes, I said. You are so beautiful.

Sabrina smiled and said this is the one I want.

Little did anyone know I was the one who would be buying this dress for her. We all walked up to the cashier after she was finished being sized and fitted for the dress. The lady rung up the dress but when she said what the price was Sabrina was shocked. Sabrina looked at the cashier and said ma'am I can't afford this dress do you have a more affordable one. Before the woman could respond I, said,

Sabrina do you like this dress?
And is this the one you want?
Yes. She replied.
Then it is settled this is the one she will have.
Here you go ma'am put it on my card.
Asia, I can't let you pay for this.
Sabrina you are my best friend and I would do
anything for you as long as you are happy that's
all that matters.
She hugged me.
Thank you.
With tears in their eyes, they smiled and held
on to each other's arms. Each one walking over
hugging me and saying thank you. I know I
have lost my damn mind but I love her that
much. I'm really starting to think I am stuck on
more than stupid. Still confused by everything,
yet the smile on her face made it all worth it.

No Regrets

Chapter 10
Spending time

It was Monday afternoon after a big meeting with one of the biggest advertising firms here in Jacksonville when I received an urgent text from Sabrina.

Hey Asia it's me can you please give me a call? ASAP

Even though the meeting was over I hadn't left the office yet. I had a chance to network with some of the agents in the office that were trying to book me for some of their private events. I couldn't afford to mess this up. Plus, Mya set this up for me and I at least owe her enough to make sure I make the most of this meeting. It was taking longer than I thought and my phone keep beeping from one text after another. I began to get worried, trying my best not to lose my nerve I booked my last event and rushed out to my car to call Sabrina. Dialing her number, I had all kids of thoughts running through my head. The phone rang.

Asia, what took you so long to call me?

Sabrina I was in a meeting and couldn't just rush out. Is everything ok with you?

No... Yes…Yes…No, I don't know.

Sabrina what's wrong? You're scaring me.

Asia, can you come and get me from my mom's house I need someone to talk to.

Sure, I'm on my way I will see you in a little while. As always when I'm nervous or super stressed I pop in my India Arie cd Voyage to India to calm my nerves. Riding to the soothing melodies to calm and ease my mind I arrive to Sabrina's mom house. I didn't even have a chance to get out the car before Sabrina came out the door. I unlocked the car door she got in.

Are you ok?

What is going on with you?

Did Marcus do something to you?

No, I think I'm just getting nervous about this wedding and not sure if I want to get married. Could it be cold feet?

I don't know I have never been engaged or married so I have no idea what emotions a person feels or the anxieties they may go through. Well let's ride down to the beach and grab a bite to eat on the water. We can talk while we eat then go for a walk right after. Sit back and just listen to some music until we get to the restaurant. Sabrina laid her seat back closed her eyes and listened to music on our ride to the beach. I have never seen her like this and I don't know if I made a mistake when she spent the night or not. I don't know where all of this is coming from. Her emotions are running amuck and raw. The truth of the matter is I don't know how to fix it. Hell, I don't even know what needs to be fixed. I'm glad that I am the person she chose to come to. Occasionally I glance over at her to see if she is ok, I'm uneasy in these moments because I don't know what to do or if there is anything I can do. We finally arrive at the restaurant. Come on let's get out. She pulls her seat up, takes off her seat belt and exit the car. She is very reserved as we are walking into the restaurant.

Good evening how many the host ask.

Two… I replied.

Would you like a table or booth?

Booth and can we get one in the back corner if you have one?

Sure, the host replied. Follow me.

We follow her to our booth.

Here you go your server will be with you shortly.

Thank you I replied.

Sabrina are you ok? I have never seen you this bothered about anything.

Yes, I'm sorry I don't mean to worry you, Asia. I am just overwhelmed about everything.

Marcus keeps calling to find out how things are going but while I'm here I really don't want to hear from him.

Why is that, Sabrina? If you don't mind me asking?

I just want to enjoy the time with everyone here and not worry about anything else. He keeps asking so many questions about the wedding.

I understand I replied. Deep in my gut I feel like there is something she isn't telling me.

How about this we can talk about whatever you want to talk about, or we can just enjoy the time together without talking as well.

Whatever you want I'm ok with that.

Thank you, Asia, for being so understanding.

No need to thank me you know I am always here for you.

Our server comes to the table.

Hi my name is Shayla I will be your server for tonight. Are you ready to order or do you need a few minutes?

Can you give us a few minutes while we look over the menu?

Not a problem. Can I get your drink orders if that's ok?

Yes, that will be fine I replied.

What will you like to drink the server asked?

Sabrina asks, can I get a sex on the beach?

Sure, and for you ma'am?

Can I get a long island ice tea?

Sure, I will be right back with your drinks.

Sabrina looks at mc as if her mind was full of questions. Something is really wrong.

What is it, Sabrina?

Tell me whatever it is that you're thinking about.

Ok, I will. She replied. Can you make love to me on the beach? Then take me back home and make love to me all night long?

I sat there for a few minutes in silence. Trying to get my thoughts together, do I really want to get myself caught up in this love triangle? Would I want someone to do this to me? She is the love of my life and my soulmate. I know what I'm doing isn't right but I can't tell her no. How can I keep doing this to Marcus? Sabrina are you sure this is what you want?

Yes, I have never been more certain.

Sabrina, your wish is my command.

I am a sucker when it comes to her.

How about we just have drinks and then go down to the beach.

I'm game with that Asia.

Sounds like a plan then, I replied.

As the server returned with our drinks, she asked if we were ready to order.

No ma'am, we are just having drinks and then we are leaving you can bring the check so we can pay.

Yes, I will be right back with that for you.

Thank you, ma'am.

Sitting there staring into each other's eyes as

we sip on our drinks, we smile so romantically at each other. I paid for the drinks we left the restaurant and began to walk down towards the beach. As we walked on the sand, we took our shoes off, place them in our hands and walk more towards the water. I took her hand in mine as we walked looking out into the moonlight bouncing off the water. Sabrina lays her head on my shoulder. With every breath I take I can taste her lips.

Suddenly we stop once Sabrina realizes we are at the end of the beach and away from everyone. We walk closer to the water sit down and let the waves wash up upon our feet. We held each other's hand, stare into each other's eyes and kiss. I lay her on her back I kiss on her neck as the waves are crashing on us. I rub my hand up her thighs and to my surprise she had no panties on. I placed my fingers inside her stroking her g-spot she moans and moans. This time I take it a step future I ease down between her legs. Pulling her pants down to her feet I slide one leg out. I lick her clit softly, sucking it with conviction and sticking my fingers inside her. Just as she began to arch her back one of the biggest waves crashed on us no need to move future up on the beach. I got up reached for her hand. As she puts her pants back on. Come on let's go home and finish what we have started. Legs shaking it took her a minute to stand up and walk. We walked back to the car soaking wet in more ways than one. I grabbed towels from the trunk and cut the heat on so we wouldn't be cold. I don't know what I was going through but it seemed to only have taken a few seconds to get home. As I pulled up in the driveway and parked, we both rushed to get out of the car. I opened the door went to the bathroom ran the water we both jumped in the shower. We started lathering each other up as the showerhead rinsed us off. I looked at her placed her legs on the wall in the shower got on my knees and picked up where I left off. She began to dig her nails in my shoulders. I cut the water off, picked her up out of the shower carried her to the bed as she wrapped her legs around my waist. I laid her on her back. I sucked on her clit as if it was the nipple of her breast. She moans, arches her back and begins to shake. I take my left hand pinch her right nipple while licking her clit and fingering her with my right hand. We become one, motion for motion, moan for moan and breath for breath. She begins to scream with passion. Oh damn, damn, freak.

You are about to make me cum. I can't hold it no longer I'm Cuming, I'm Cuming.

As her juices flow, I suck them all up not letting one drop hit the sheets. She holds my head in place as she reaching her climax.

Asia come and hold me please.

I came up behind her in the bed and held her as if I was scared to let her go. That night I did what I wanted to do for years since I first met her and that was to give her all of my love, mind, body and soul. As we laid there and she drifted off to sleep I had no idea of what I was getting myself into. Am I setting myself up? How would Marcus feel about this if he finds out? But all of that were worries for another day.

No Regrets

Chapter 11
She returns home

It had been a few weeks since Sabrina had returned back home to New York. I still haven't heard from her and she won't answer my calls or text. I'm starting to feel like I made a huge mistake by crossing that line with my best friend. Sitting in my office looking out the window I feel so lost and confused. Sabrina's bachelorette party is just weeks away. I'm so afraid that even though I planned everything in New York I'm not sure if she still wants me to attend. Feeling like I just lost my love and best-friend. I haven't been taking care of my business the way I should. I haven't spent much time with Mya. Guilt became me. Despair held me. Confusion fed me. Feeling like I was in a sunken place. I know I can't afford to lose any clients. Neither can I take things further with Mya. I could never give her my all. She deserves someone who can, right now that just isn't me. The times we share are amazing, but she would only get a fraction of me. How can such an incredible and phenomenal woman come into my life while I'm still in love with someone else. Damn, how did I get here? In that moment I thought I couldn't find my way out of this dark place then my phone rang. Hello…

Hey baby, how's my grandbaby doing? My grandmother asked.

Hey grandma, I'm ok, I guess.

What's wrong sugar?

It's Sabrina I haven't heard from her since she went back home and I don't know if I have ruined my friendship.

Ruined it how baby?

You know I can't control myself or my feelings when I'm with Sabrina and we crossed that line. I lose all sense of reason when I'm around her. Needless to say, we were intimate more than once. I don't know if this is why she is ignoring me.

I'm sure she will contact you soon Asia. I doubt that this has ruined things between you two.

Grandma I'm supposed to go to New York for her bridal party but I don't know if I should still go. She wouldn't let me get a hotel and I'm supposed to stay with her and Marcus. How can I even look him in the eye knowing that I had sex with his fiancé? Not only that but he is my friend as well.

Oh, baby you are being too hard on yourself. Just breathe I'm sure things will work out.

Grandma, what do I do about Mya?

What do you mean baby?

I know where Mya stands with me. But I know I can't give her my all. But I really like her.

Just be honest with her baby, I'm sure she will understand. She is a different kind of woman. A good one I must add. But only you know your heart. You know what you want. You and Mya make a great couple but you will only love one woman. Only time will tell don't stress too much baby. Get yourself together come over I'm fixing your favorite for dinner and I know Maria will be happy to see you.

Ok grandma I will see you shortly.

I love you baby.

I love you too grandma.

I must say having dinner with my grandma and Mrs. Maria will make me feel better. Also listening to their words of wisdom always comforts me.

Thank God for the elders.

Later that night when I got home, I decided to have me a glass of wine and some good ole jazz to ease my mind after dinner. When my phone rang.

Hello.

Asia.

This is she, who's calling?

Miguel.

Well hello stranger, how have you been? It's good to hear from you.

I'm good just wanted to call you since Sabrina told me that you asked about me.

Did she now. So, what do I owe this call?

Are you still coming for Sabrina's bachelorette party?

Yes, why you ask?

You haven't heard?

Heard what Miguel?

I think you should come up here so you can find out for yourself?

Find out what Miguel?

Damn, Asia. I knew I shouldn't have called but you will find out sooner or later. I shouldn't be the one to tell you but what the hell.

Tell me what Miguel?

Sabrina is pregnant.

Pregnant I whispered.

Yes, but I don't think Marcus is happy about the news. I take it you haven't heard from her since she's been back.

No, I haven't now I know why. What made you tell me this?

I know you two are best friends and she really needs someone right now.

I've reached out to her but Miguel I can't get her to answer any of my calls. Can you tell her to call me?

If I do then I will have to tell her I told you what is going on.

So, what's wrong with that?

I'm not sure if she wanted you to know. Every time I told her to call you, she stared crying and

I can't understand why. Asia, I will tell her to
call you but please whatever
you say or do be easy on her.
I will, I promise. Thank you for telling me,
Miguel. I appreciate it.
You're welcome! Asia, I miss you and I wish
we could have worked out.
I miss you too Miguel, you know we are better
as friends and I will always be here for you.
I know Asia, talk to you later.
Talk to you later.
I sat there heartbroken, torn, I felt betrayed and
used. Was this karma coming back on me
already? How could she sleep with me when
she is pregnant from Marcus? How can she
look me in my eye and lie to me about not
sleeping with him? Or how could she just go
back to him and sleep with him right after
making love to me? Am I a fool
for loving her? Was I just a last fling?
How can she be so damn selfish? I can't lie I
miss her. No matter how much it hurts I still
want to be with her. She is the only one that can
fill this empty place within me. I sound like a
damn fool. Stupid and desperate for allowing
this to happen. She is playing with me and with

Marcus. How can I love someone like this? I look over at the clock it's too later to call my grandma but I'm hoping Mrs. Maria is still up. I dial Mrs. Maria's number as the phone rang, I got nervous. As I'm about to hang up, I hear Hola Asia.

Hello Mrs. Sanchez.

What's wrong baby are you ok?

No ma'am.

What is it?

It's Sabrina.

What about Sabrina?

She won't answer my calls and I don't know what I have done to make her feel like she has to ignore me.

Asia it's not you, she is going through some things right now and the last person she wants to upset or hurt is you. She feels like if she doesn't talk to you then she doesn't have to hear the hurt in your voice.

But Ma, why can't she just be honest with me? Why did I have to find out from someone else what is going on with my best friend? Regardless if it hurts or not that will not stop me from being there for her it never has.

I know Asia, I tried to tell her that but she

won't listen to me.

I understand, I will just have to wait to see if or when she will call. I love her and will always be here for her.

Asia baby, whenever you do talk to her ask her to tell you the whole story so that you can decide for yourself if you will really stay or go.

Is it that bad ma?

I'm afraid it is mi amor. She has really gotten herself in a mess this time. I know how much you love her Asia. But don't allow yourself any unnecessary pain. Please get some rest and come by tomorrow so we can talk more.

Yes, ma'am I love you and good night.

I love you too Asia, good night.

No Regrets

Chapter 12
The Bachelorette Party

I finally arrive in New York and Miguel has agreed to meet me at the airport. As I am walking to baggage claim I am getting more and more anxious. I have no clue as to what I am about to walk into. The conversation I had with Sabrina's mom lingers in my head. This was supposed to be a loving trip where I get to enjoy my friends and see New York. Now not so much. How can I look at Marcus while sleeping in his house after having sex with Sabrina? How am I going to be able to be there for my best friend knowing she has lied to me in some form or fashion. Also, I can't help but to wonder how Miguel fits into this web of lies. But I am about to find out before I meet up with

Sabrina and Marcus.

Asia.

I heard my name being called. I turned around it was Miguel. If I were into men, he would most defiantly be the man of my dreams. Cute, fine, caring, loving and handsome makes you want to eat him up. Maybe he could be my child's father I know he wouldn't mind. At least for him that would keep us bonded. I smiled and walked towards him standing there smiling like a kid in a candy store. We embrace, we give each other a friendly kiss and walk out the airport. He opens the door to his car and we drive off. Miguel.

Yes, Asia.

Please be honest with me so I can have some kind of a clue of what I am walking into.

I will do my best.

What is truly going on with Sabrina? I know you know so don't bullshit me. I can't get her to open up to me and you are my last hope of finding out.

Oh, Asia. Damn it. Please don't make me tell you.

Miguel you better start talking before I bust you upside your head. And pray to God we don't wreck.

Ok, damn girl you don't have to get physical.

What I am about to tell you may set you on fire.
I am asking your forgiveness in advance.

Forgiveness…Damn it, Miguel. Just tell me already.

Ok, here goes nothing he said right before he dropped a bomb on me.

Well, you know Sabrina has never been with a man or anyone for that matter right.

Right, I said.

As my heart felt like it was going to beat out of my chest.

Sabrina called me one night so that we could talk she asked me for a favor. I hate to tell you this, but the favor was for me to be her first so that she would know what it felt like to be with another man before she got married. I told her no at first because of how I felt about you. But she was so desperate and wouldn't let it go. So, we went back and forth until I decided to do it. Not thinking we didn't use protection. That next day her and Marcus slept together they used protection but the condom broke. She later found out she was pregnant but wasn't sure who the father was. The only reason why I called you was so that you wouldn't think anything less of me. But I guess that backfired. Miguel, please tell me you aren't serious right now? How could you? How could she? How did you think I would feel about this? Marcus is your best friend. I was the one you wanted Miguel. You were the one man I felt could be the father of my child one day despite us not being together. Did anyone consider how I would feel? Hell, how Marcus would feel. Yet here I am in the middle of some bullshit. I can't believe I came knowing that something was wrong.

Damn it… looking out the window feeling dead on the inside. I just want to punch the shit out of him right now. It is Sabrina who I really should be mad at for starting all of this nonsense. Agony beats upon my heart. Miguel, can you do me a favor?

Anything for you Asia.

Can you take me somewhere to have a stiff drink so I can get my head together?

I can't be mad at you Miguel but I am disappointed with you. I don't know how long it will take for me to get over this hurt. Please believe me when I say I am so sorry

Asia. The last thing I wanted to do was hurt you or Marcus. I don't know how I am supposed to stand next to him as his best man knowing that I may be the father of his fiancé's baby. Miguel, what I do know this situation is all kinds of wrong. For now, I will lean on you and you can lean on me until this is over and we will find out where to go from here. We arrived at some bar. I was so disarrayed I didn't have a clue as to where we were. He parked we got out of the car and walked in. Miguel pulled my chair out for me and ordered drinks. I just sat there holding my head in my hands. Sabrina had no reason to tell me the untruth. We never lied to each other but said what we had to even if it hurt. Tears in my eyes, confused and hurt beyond understanding. I looked up at him and tossed my drink back. He ordered me another I tossed that one back as well. My soul was dying, burning in my own pain. He just looked at me with pain in his eyes. I sat there for a few minutes glanced back at him with so much hurt, pain and a pinch of hate in my eyes. Drowning in my tears. Thinking to myself Asia pull yourself together and just get past the next few days. I couldn't be more relieved that the bachelorette dinner is tomorrow night.

Come on Miguel I think I'm ready to go.

He paid the tab; we walk out the bar got into the car and headed to Marcus and Sabrina's home. We pull up to the house, Miguel grabbed my bags and we walked up to the door. I rang the doorbell. The door opened it was Marcus. He let me in and gave me a hug.

Asia I'm so glad to see you, Sabrina has been crying and she's just been out of it. I'm glad you are here so that you can be here for her.

Marcus, you know all you have to do is call and I will be here for you guys.

Marcus showed me to the room where Sabrina was.

I know you will Asia. Go in, Marcus said.

I hugged him then knocked on the door before walking in. Hey best friend, I said as I sat on the bed. Sabrina began to cry as she heard my voice. Sabrina look at me.

Sabrina… she turned around and sat up in the bed. Her head hung as she just sat there.

Asia I am so sorry, I didn't mean to hurt you. You are the last person I wanted to bring any pain to.

I took her and held her in my arms. I rubbed her head and said it's ok I love you no matter what. You know we are better than anything that comes up against us. But Sabrina I have to ask what is the whole story? Don't leave nothing out.

She looked at me as tears form again in her eyes.

I lied to you about why Marcus kept calling me. I lied to you about not sleeping with anyone. I slept with Miguel after guilting him into it, then I slept with Marcus and later found out I was pregnant. Marcus doesn't want to have any kids right now and wants me to have an abortion. He says kids doesn't fit into the plan right now. I want to only because I'm not sure if it is Marcus or Miguel's baby.

Sabrina, you will do no such thing. If it wasn't meant for you to have a baby you would have never gotten pregnant. If at any moment you feel like you don't want this child, I will take care of it. But you will not have a damn abortion. Do you hear me?

Yes.

Asia, how can you be so loving when you know

I have lied and hurt you?

Sabrina one thing that you haven't learned is love is not selfish. So, until you learn that you will never understand. Let's just get you through the next two days and we will worry about everything else later. She laid back in the bed I laid behind her until she fell asleep.

I walked into the kitchen where Marcus and Miguel were having drinks.

Hey can I get one of those?

Sure…

Asia how is Sabrina?

She is still upset but she will be fine once she wakes up.

Asia thank you; I have been trying to calm her down for days but I knew once you came, she would be alright. You two are more like sisters than best friends and no matter what she can always call on you Asia.

We all are like family Marcus and you all know I will be here for either one of you, guys.

Yeah, you right. Marcus stated.

Well, you guys it is getting late and I am a little tired from my flight. Marcus can you show me to my room?

Sure. Here you go Asia. Everything you need is in the room and there is a bathroom in your room as well. Sleep tight and see you in the morning.

Marcus closes the door behind him, I can't help but feel terrible. Here I am in this man house knowing I have been sleeping with his fiancé. Despite how betrayed I feel about the things Sabrina has done I still love her and want to be here for her. Feeling guilty isn't going to make this visit any easier. I put my suitcase on the bed to pull out my pajamas so that I can take a nice hot shower and get some rest. I walk into the bathroom turn the shower water on. As I take my clothes off, I look at myself in the mirror not believing what I see. A tear drops my eye, I wipe my face and get in the shower. Thinking that if I can just freshen up, I would feel better. But who was I trying to fool, I cannot change what has happened and this shower was not making me feel any better. So, I just finished washing up and sucked the past up. I got out, dried off, lotion up put my pajamas on and got in bed. Before I knew it, I fell fast asleep. When I awoke the next morning, I had a few things to make sure was taken care of for the bridal dinner. Eating breakfast and seeing Marcus and Miguel off was by far the hardest thing to do. This man cooked for me and here I am sexing his soon to be wife. After making a few phone calls the next task would be even harder getting Sabrina ready for her own bridal dinner. Thankfully the only people in the house was Sabrina and myself. Marcus went to hang out with Miguel and the boys for one last hurrah. Sabrina has been a mess since she found out she was pregnant. Now is the time for her to get her act together because we are having a simple dinner with Marcus family. God knows they don't need to find out what is going on. She didn't want to have anything big since all this took place. I took a deep breath walked over to Sabrina's room and knocked on the door.

Sabrina it's me can I come in?

Yes.

As I opened the door, I walked in to find Sabrina sitting on the side of the bed looking a hot mess. Sabrina why haven't you done anything with yourself?

She just looked and me and shook her head.

Well, miss thang do you plan on getting ready

for this dinner?

Asia, how can I? Marcus is really mad with me and I still haven't told him the truth and to be honest I don't know if I will. The last thing I wanted to do was hurt anyone. But look at this mess I've gotten myself in. I've hurt you, used Miguel and lied to Marcus. Tell me why should I go through with this wedding?

Let me ask you this Sabrina, do you still love Marcus?

Of course, I do Asia you know that.

Do you still feel like he is your forever?

Yes.

Does he still love you?

Yes.

Ok then, now get your ass up and get ready. I will tell you this Sabrina it will be better for Marcus to find out about the baby from you rather than from someone else. I mean I'm not going to say anything but you know Miguel can't hold water when he starts drinking that's all I'm saying. You handle it the best way you see fit because it's your life. I will be here no matter what to help you pick up the pieces. Now get up take a shower get dressed so we can go ma'am.

I just hope Sabrina will be ok. I sat on the bed thinking to myself this is going to be a long freaking night. I pray she can keep it together. The last thing she needs is to fall apart and Marcus family finds out what is going on. Damn…I need to hurry up and get my ass back home to Florida. I guess I won't be seeing New York on this trip. Or doing any shopping. This I must say has been a trip for the books.

No Regrets

Chapter 13
I Do

The big day has finally arrived for Sabrina and Marcus September 24th. As I'm standing here watching Sabrina get her makeup done, I can't help but feel like a proud friend and sister. We have gone through so much but I must admit I am truly happy for her. I didn't know how I would feel when this day would arrive. Believe it or not I am good. I just hope that she doesn't act shady once she sees that I invited Mya to be my plus one for the wedding. The photographer finally came in to take pictures of her before the wedding. I stood back leaning against the wall smiling because Sabrina does make a beautiful bride. Her beautiful brown eye, full lips, and beautiful smile gets me every time. Her mother, her grandmother and my grandmother sat on the couch with big smiles on their faces while holding hands. Now that her makeup is done it's time for her to get her hair done. We only have about forty-five minutes before the wedding starts. As she is finishing up, I unzip her garment bag and take her wedding dress out so I can help her get ready. Alright miss thang let's get you in this dress so we can get you down this aisle to your future husband. Sabrina walks over to me slips her dress on and turns around so that I can zip up her dress.

Ma, can you please come put the veil on your baby?

Sure, I can. Sabrina baby I am so happy for you. You look so beautiful.

She hugs Sabrina then pins the veil on her head then flips it over her face. Grandma walks over gives Sabrina a hug her grandmother does the same and then they exit the dressing room.

Are you ready?

Yes, Asia thank you for being here for me. I don't know what I would have done without you.

You are quite welcome my friend. I love you and you know I will always be here for you. We walk out as everyone is lining up to get ready to walk down the aisle. First to walk in is the pastor, then Marcus then the best man Miguel. There was no bridesmaids or groomsmen just the best man and the maid of honor which is me of course. I walk down the aisle next, once I took my place the music started to play. All my life was the song she would walk in on. Accompanied by her mother on one side and my grandmother on the other. They walked her down the aisle to give her away. I looked over at Marcus to see what facial expression he had on his face. His eyes began to fill with tears no matter what has happened I know he loves her and would do anything for her. Marcus walked over to take Sabrina by the hand as they took their places. The wedding began and you could just feel the love in the room. Sabrina read her vows first, she cried and even got choked up a few times. Marcus would wipe away her tears while fighting back his own. Now it was his turn. With raw emotions on his face, I began to wonder if he would be able to go through with this. With tears running down his face she wipes them away. He carries on, getting choked up, in that moment there isn't a dry eye in the house. Once he finished, he looked at Sabrina with so much love and passion in his eyes and whispered I love you. As they exchange rings the pastor announces" I now pronounce you husband and wife you may now kiss the bride. I had never seen them kiss so hard and lovingly. The pastor walked down the aisle first. They took each other's hands, walked down the aisle. Miguel took my hand as we followed, then everyone else. The wedding guest headed to the reception hall while we went outside to finish taking pictures. Once that was over, we made our way to the reception hall. The doors opened they announced me and Miguel. The DJ then yelled; I now present to you Mr. and Mrs. Marcus Brown.

Everyone cheered, come to the dance floor for the first dance you two the DJ said over the mic. They danced as they held each other laughing, talking and gazing at each other. Dancing in pure bliss, happiness and solace. Once the first dance was over the servers began bringing out everyone's meal.

Many were still at the open bar and I looked
over and saw Miguel drinking more than
enough of his share. I walked up to him.
Miguel are you ok?
He shook his head yes and kept drinking.
Torment overcame him, looking as if his life
was coming to an end. A cloud of regret
hovered over him. Miguel why don't you come
and sit with us so we can give the toast?
He took my hand as we walked over to where
we were sitting. Clink, clink, clink. Miguel
stood up to give a toast.
Can I have everyone's attention. I'm not good
at this but I just want to wish these two a happy
and blessed union. I have seen this relationship
blossom and I don't know of any two more
deserving of love then these two
congratulations Marcus and Sabrina.
Asia, would you please stand it's your turn.
I smiled, thank you Miguel.
Marcus and Sabrina, I must admit when you
two became an item I thought I was going to
lose my best friend and I didn't like you at first
Marcus. But over time I saw how happy you
made Sabrina and that made it easier to let my
friend go. The more you two showed your love

for each other I realized I wasn't losing my friend but I was gaining a brother. Just know that as long as you two communicate in good times and bad times and keep others out of your marriage. Keep God first. You two will be ok. To my brother and sister, I love you both and so thankful to be here in this moment to share in such a beautiful love and occasion. May God continue to strengthen and bless your union. Let's raise our glasses to Marcus and Sabrina. How can I give such a warm, loving speech knowing what I have done? I have got to be the biggest hypocrite. I sat down after giving the toast to finish eating. Miguel and I talked as the newlyweds mingled with the guest. Some were out on the dance floor and we all were having a good time. Miguel and I walked to the dance floor danced and laughed like the good ole times. Then Marcus grabbed my grandmothers hand and Sabrina's mom hand and brought them over to the dance floor. Marcus danced with Mrs. Maria and Miguel danced with my grandmother while Sabrina and I stood watching them. Sabrina and I walked over to the dance floor and cut in I was dancing with my grandmother and Sabrina was dancing with her mother. There was nothing but love and smiles in the room. As we walked them back over to their seats, I saw Miguel drinking now more than before. I'm thinking to myself I'm so glad that this night is almost over. But what I didn't see was Miguel and Marcus arguing. I saw Marcus grab Sabrina by the arm as they walked out of the reception hall. I followed to make sure everything would be ok. As I look out of the crack, I made in the door I could hear Marcus asking Sabrina if she had slept with Miguel. Rage vibrated from every ounce of Marcus being. Remembering moments before made me realize why Miguel was drinking so much. Sabrina, standing there looking like a child being scolded she began crying hysterically but there was nothing I could do this time.

Tell me Sabrina is that my baby Marcus yelled. Is that my baby you're carrying Sabrina? Sabrina crouched forward grabbing her stomach. Yelled call 911.

Sabrina passed out. Rushing through the doors I ran over to her as Marcus reached in his pocket for his cell phone to call 911.

I kneeled down over Sabrina.

Sabrina wake up baby, I patted her face.
Sabrina wake up for me, come on Sabrina
please wake up baby. Tears covered my
face, frantic and panicking. By this time, her
mom had run out the reception hall followed
by my grandmother and her grandmother.
Asia, honey move let her mom in come here.
I moved as Mrs. Maria knelled down over
Sabrina.
Asia, sugar what happened?
Grandma I will tell you but not right now. I
promise I will I just need to make sure Sabrina
is going to be ok.
Sirens blared echoing through the halls. The
ambulance finally got there the paramedics
rushed in with the gurney. They kneeled over
her to see if she had a pulse and if she was
breathing. Seeing a moment where she opened
her eyes for a split second. They put an oxygen
mask over her face while getting information
on what had happened. They placed her on the
gurney and rushed her to the hospital. Marcus
rode in the ambulance with her. Mya standing
there looking at me. Mya, can I call you later.
Yes, she replied. I grabbed my keys rushed out
as I drove my car following them. Arriving at

the ER, I dropped everyone off so that I could find a place to park. Thinking to myself what does Mya think of me. I found the first empty parking space and sat in my car and cried. I said a quick prayer so I could pull myself together.

Oh God watch over Sabrina, please let her be alright. She has made some mistakes but don't take her. Not now. I know you have it under control. I'm trusting in you. Hear my plea. Amen.

I got out the car and headed for the entrance to the ER. The stench of sickness and despair filled the air in the hospital. I watched for a second as everyone was just sitting there, some praying while waiting to hear from the doctor. Marcus was pacing back and forth, hands folded up to his mouth but with a weird look on his face. I walked up to him to see if he was ok.
Marcus how are you holding up?
As I gave him a hug, he looked down at me.
Asia, I don't know how I'm feeling right now.
I understand my friend. Come take a walk with me since it will be a while before the doctors

come out to let us know what is going on.
Asia, I don't know if I should be angry or
hurt or simply be here for my wife. What
Miguel told me about the two of them I just
don't know if I can get past it. I'm hurt,
betrayed and disappointed by them both.
Miguel being my best friend he knew better.
Sabrina being the one I want to spend my life
with. She should have never put us here in this
situation. Damn, Asia. I just don't know how to
feel right now. I see why she was in such a rush
to go back home when
she told me she was pregnant.
Marcus how far along is Sabrina?
She should be a few months. But to be
honest I don't know. Sabrina knew I wasn't
ready for any kids but now I don't even know if
this kid is mine.
As I'm listening to Marcus telling me how he is
feeling I can't help but to think of how she lied
to me. Her and Miguel both. Yet I'm standing
here swallowing my guilt.
Marcus, do you love Sabrina?
Asia, you know I do? Why would you ask me
something you know the answer to?
If you still love her and she is still your

everything then you can move past this. It may take some time but I know it can happen. We all make mistakes but we are only human. We don't always do what's right out of fear or whatever reason. I'm not justifying or condoning this. Marcus promise me that you will think and pray about this before you make a decision.

I promise I will Asia, thank you for being here for me.

No thanks needed. You would do the same for me. Let's go back and see if the doctor has some news for us.

Let's go. Marcus said as he placed his arms around my shoulder.

With every step we took I felt more and more pain from the lies Sabrina has told me. Yet the agony of the truth I haven't told Marcus weighs even heavier on my shoulders. His arms felt like bricks being stacked on my shoulder from me not being honest with him. I just don't feel it's my place to tell him what happened. But at this moment it's not about me but about my friends. I just have to suck it up until I am able to talk to Sabrina one on one. As we walked into the waiting room the doctor came

out to talk to us and give an update on Sabrina.
Mr. Brown your wife is just fine but
unfortunately, she lost the baby.
You can go in to see her if you would like.
Yes, doc I would love to go see my wife.
Marcus turned around and said does anyone
else want to come in with me. Mrs. Maria, her
grandmother and my grandmother got up.
Asia, are you coming?
No, you all go in and I will go see her once you
guys come out.
Are you sure? Marcus asked.
Yes, Marcus, I'm sure. I just need a minute.
Ok, I will be out to get you in a few.
Ok, thanks.
I sat in the chair with such a heavy heart and
broken spirit. I didn't know if I could even face
Sabrina. How could she lie to me? We never
lied to each other nor did we keep secrets. My
love for her has become a thorn in my side.
How can I keep doing this to myself? What
does she really think about me? How does she
really feel about me?
It began to feel as if time was standing still
and I was weighed down in grief. Troubled
with so many thoughts and emotions. Disbelief,

disappointment, heartache, betrayal and confusion sat with me lying in the pool of tears in my hand.

Finally, everyone came back. I got up and headed for Sabrina's room. Marcus walked me to the door then turned back around. I walked in and closed the door. How are you feeling?

I feel ok but more so relieved?

Relieved? Why is that, Sabrina?

Yes, relieved because I had no idea who my child's father was and I couldn't stomach hurting Marcus if it had been Miguel's baby.

I'm glad that you are ok. But are you thinking of anyone else other than yourself?

Asia, what's wrong with you?

Is there something you'd like to tell me Sabrina?

What do you mean Asia?

Sabrina, did you or did you not know that you were pregnant when you came home?

Sabrina sat there looking like a deer in headlights. Busted not saying a word as tears formed in her eyes.

Are you going to answer me?

This may not come out right but I meant you no malice. I had a feeling I was pregnant; I only took one of those home pregnancy tests and had yet to go to the doctors to find out for sure. But I hadn't slept with anyone in a while before you and I slept together.

Sabrina, are you hearing yourself right now? You lied to me saying you hadn't slept with anyone. To top it all off you had me slopping up behind not one but two different men. That is some foul shit. You didn't appreciate or respect me enough or love me enough to tell me the truth. Anger and rage made my blood boil. If I didn't love her, I would beat the daylights out of her. But I respect and lover her more than that. Well, I'm glad you no longer have to hurt Marcus. But I can't say you didn't hurt me. I guess it was easier hurting me more than anyone else. Knowing I would be here no matter how bad you treated me. Or so you thought. I don't know if I can get over this. I love you but I can't right now. I turned towards the door.

Asia....

I kept walking.

Asia...

Not once looking back I walked to the waiting room. I gave everyone a hug and left. My grandmother, her grandmother, Mrs. Maria and Marcus kept calling my name. The tears began to flow from my eyes. And I couldn't let anyone see me cry anymore. How many tears do I have to shed before I get it? Once I heard Asia Marie Dupree, I knew my grandmother was serious. I stopped and just stood there. I heard my grandmother footsteps get closer and closer.

Asia, turn around.

No, grandma I can't, please don't make me.

Asia, what is wrong with you? As she walked in front of me and raised my head up with her hands.

She saw the tears running like rivers from my eyes. She just wrapped her arms around me and placed my head upon her chest. She could tell that I was beyond hurt.

Come sit with me baby.

We walked over to another waiting area.

Baby, are you going to be ok?

Grandma, I don't know this time. Sabrina looked me in my eyes on more than one occasion and lied to me. How could she do that to me? I'm in a position where I haven't lied to Marcus but I haven't been honest with him.

Baby, sometimes when we are afraid of losing someone, we will do some stupid
things.
Grandma, she might just lose me any way.
She had no reason to lie. You know I can't
stand a liar and she lied to me. Grandma, how
am I supposed to feel? You were right
sometimes you just have to let go. I have to let
her go she has hurt me to my soul and I don't
know if I can forgive her for that. I will be in
the car whenever you guys are ready to go.
Take your time and I love you.
I love you too baby.
I got up and walked out so that I could be alone
with my pain before we all left to head home.

No Regrets

Chapter 14
How could she

Days later I woke up still hurting. Head pounding, eyes swollen from all the crying every day and night. Mourning drenched the air; black clouds seem to hover over me. Regret consumed me but I can't let this stop me from living. I just keep thinking about how Sabrina lied to my face when all I ever did was be honest with her. Hell, I probably would have still slept with her anyway. At least Mya understood when I called and explained everything to her and we will remain friends. I walked into the bathroom to wash my face and brush my teeth when I heard a knock at the door. I rinsed out my mouth and headed to the front door.

Who is it?

Sabrina.

I just stood there not knowing if I was going to open the door or not.

Asia, please let me in. Please…

Sabrina, what do you want?

I need to speak with you, just hear me out.

I unlocked the door then walked away. As she walked in, I couldn't even look at her. What could be so important that she needs to say? Better yet will she tell me another lie. How can I believe anything she has to say anymore?

Asia, I know you may feel as if you can't believe anything I say. But please know I love you and that I am so sorry that I hurt you. I never meant to hurt you but I thought if you knew the truth that you wouldn't have given me what I needed and that was to feel the passion of your love for me.

It's always about you Sabrina.

Don't be like that Asia. You are the only one that I can honestly say loves me without conditions and limitations. I took that for granted and even though I don't deserve your love please don't take that from me.

You are a piece of work Sabrina. Here you stand in my house asking me not to take my love from you while you are married to someone else. While you slept with other people and lied to me about that.

Sabrina do you even know what you want? Do you know what you want from me?

Tell me this, why did you marry Marcus?

Asia, to be honest I thought I knew why but I really don't. I love him and I know he loves me but the feelings aren't as deep for him as they are for you.

Oh, now you have feelings for me Mrs. Brown.

If you had feelings for me, you would have never married someone else. You would have stayed here with me when you came back home. Better yet you would have never left. And regardless to who the father of your baby was I would have loved the baby as if it was mine. You know why... because I love you just that much. But once again for Sabrina that wasn't good enough. So, I guess you want me to sit around and wait for you to decide whether you do or don't want to be with Marcus anymore. You have got a set of cast-iron balls.

At what point are you going to stop playing with me? You know my feelings, that has never been an issue.

But can you see yourself being the wife of a woman? Can you?

Asia, I don't know.

I know you don't that's why you married Marcus. Call the thing a thing stand in it and own it, Sabrina. Damn… Learn to first be honest with yourself before trying to be honest with me. Sabrina, I love you and always will but I won't keep putting my life on hold waiting for you. While you continue to play with me while trying to figure it out.

Besides Marcus is a good man and he deserves someone who can give him the same in return of what he is giving them.

Asia, you are so right. I need to learn to be honest with myself but in being honest with myself I ended up hurting those I love the most. I know I need to make some decisions but I'm confused. If I go with my heart then I will hurt Marcus but if I go with my comfort, I will hurt you again. I don't want to hurt you any more than I already have. I wish I could turn back the hands of time but I can't. I'm at a lost right now.

Sabrina, my friend, my love I can't help you decide this is something you have to do on your own. Also, this is something you should have figured out before getting

married. Does Marcus know about you and me?

Yes, he asked me why you were so upset when you left out of the hospital room and I told him everything. The thing that surprised me was that he always knew how you felt about me and wasn't upset when I told him we slept together. He said he knew it would have happened eventually. But then he asked me if I loved you the same way I loved him. When I said yes that's what hurt him. I was honest with him when I told him I loved you more. He still wants the marriage but I'm not sure if it will ever be what we both thought it would be.

Well, Sabrina you have a decision you have to make. I suggest you put your big girl panties on and do what you feel is best for you before you lose out all the way around. I can't anymore. Either we are going to work past this in efforts to be together or not. You decide if you can ever be the wife of a woman. If you can't then you need to figure out if you can give Marcus what he deserves or let him move on and find someone who will. Let me do the same. I love you but this web of lies that you have created has become more than I can bare. This has become too toxic. To be honest Sabrina I don't know if I want you in my life anymore.

Sabrina stood there in shock crying.

Asia I can't live without you and I'm not willing to do so.

She reaches out for my hand and I notice there is no ring on her ring finger.

Sabrina what is going on with you and Marcus.

Asia, I know things will never be the same with Marcus and I so I couldn't continue to be his wife. We are getting the marriage dissolved that's why I am here. I can live without him but I can't live without you. I'm in love with you Asia and always have been but I was too scared of what others would say. Instead of focusing on the love we have for each other. I'm yours Asia if you are willing to have me.

No Regrets

Chapter 15
No Regrets

The sun shined bright through the window curtains the next morning, I awoke with Sabrina in my arms. As I lay there looking at her angelic, peaceful and beautiful face as she slept. My heart just melted all over again. We spent most of the night talking and trying to figure things out. There were a lot of swearing, tears, yelling, screaming, door slamming, pain and hurt. But I feel I owe it to myself to at least try and see where things go with the both of us. If I couldn't be part of the solution then I had to be part of the problem but I wasn't going to give up without a fight. I kissed Sabrina on the forehead.

Wake up sleepy head, I whispered in her ear. She smiled and caressed my face with her hand. Good morning Asia.

Good morning my love. Would you like some breakfast?

Yes, I would love some.

Great let me get up and cook us a bite to eat, I will be back in a few. By the way would you like orange juice or apple juice with your breakfast?

Orange juice will be fine.

I got out of bed brushed my teeth, washed my face and headed to the kitchen. No matter what it is I am doing I have to play music. Picked up the remote to the cd player

and let the melodic melodies of smooth jazz fill the air. In the kitchen cooking omelets, squeezing juice, wondering can I be crazy thinking Sabrina could really be my baby. Through it all we have always been there for each other, plus the love is real. Screw it, I will ride this ride as long as I can until it ends. I plated up our food and put them on trays to head back to the bedroom. As I walk through the door Sabrina sits up in the bed.

Something smells good.

Only for you my love, I have some turkey bacon, spinach, tomatoes, onions and cheese omelets, with wheat toast and avocado and some fresh squeezed orange juice.

Thank you, Asia.

Can I ask you a question?

Sure, what's up?

Do you see yourself marrying me, Asia?

I sat there for a minute looking confused.

Yes, you're the only one I ever wanted to marry. Why do you ask?

Asia, for once I can see what you have always seen. I love you more than life itself and I want to marry you and start a family with you.

Sabrina, with everything we talked about last night into the early morning you never once told me this. Why all of a sudden you want to marry me and start a family with me?

Asia, I knew my mother would understand and support me no matter what but I wasn't sure if the rest of my family would.

So, I made a decision based on what I thought my family would support. Doing so I almost lost the one person that loved me and that I loved with all that I am.

Damn, I never knew you felt this way. Sabrina, I knew you loved me but I didn't think you felt as strongly for me as I do you. Despite all we have been through there is no one other than you I would want to go to sleep next to at night and wake up next to in the morning. Heavens know I would go through this all over again if I knew it would bring you back to me.

We sat on the bed ate our breakfast while the sounds of jazz played in the background. She looked into my eyes as I looked back into hers. The moment couldn't get any better than this. Sabrina got up walked over to my side of the bed where I was sitting kneeled down reached between the mattress pulled out a diamond ring and to my surprise, she asked me to marry her. The tears of joy flowed from my eyes and I felt as if the wind was just knocked out of my sails. As she held my hand with one hand and the ring in the other hand, I got myself together and said yes.

She smiled and began crying.

She got up off her knee leaned in to kiss me and laid me on my back. She slid the breakfast

tray to the side wrapped her left arm around me
and slid me up further unto the bed. She then
pulled my shirt over my head, gently kissing
my breast, neck and lips. No matter how many
times she and I made love I was always the
giver. To my surprise this day I was about to
receive all the love I have ever wanted form
her. Her lips felt like silk against my skin. Her
tongue warm and smooth like melted butter on
my nipples. As she reaches over on the tray and
grabs the glass of orange juice. She makes a
path of juice from my neck to my navel,
sucking the juice from my body. She removes
her clothes as we lay side by side naked flesh
against flesh holding each other.
Then she slides her hand between my legs
rubbing my clit. I began to moan, wetter and
wetter I became as she strokes my clit. Kissing
my body so softly, from my neck to my navel
to the top of my womb of life. Her warm
tongue gently strokes my clit as I feel my
temperature rise. Sucking and licking so
seductively my back arches. I give into her with
all my mind, body and soul. We become one as
I reach my climax. In sync she reaches hers as
well. This went on for hours as we took our

time pleasing each other. Moring turned to noon; noon turns to night. I pull her up to me, kiss her then turn her back to me as we lie there spooning. I kiss her neck. Never have I ever until that moment been physically, mentally, spiritually and emotionally satisfied.

We fell asleep that night in each other's arm with no regrets or misunderstandings.

The next day we decided to tell our family about our engagement.

Good morning my beautiful fiancé!

Good morning my beautiful wife to be, Sabrina replied.

Let's get up so we can go and share the good news with our family.

We both got up and went to take a shower only to my surprise we would pick up where we left off from last night. I must admit there was more going on in that shower than steam. Sabrina had surprised me once more with making love to me. She knew that there was no way that I would ever be able to turn her down. I marveled at the fact that she was mine and that I was hers and with every chance we would let each other know.

Finally, we finished with our shower got

dressed and headed to my grandmother's house since Sabrina's mom was already over there. We pulled up in the driveway gave each other a kiss and got out of the car. I had my own key so there was no reason to knock. As I opened the door I heard.

Asia, is that you baby?

Yes, grandma it's me.

Come on in, Maria and I are just sitting here talking. Have you seen Sabrina?

Yes, ma'am she is with me.

Good morning, Sabrina said with a smile.

Good morning, they responded.

We all gave each other hugs and kisses.

Asia baby what is this glow I see on the both of your faces?

Well, we have something to tell you.

Spit it out, don't keep us waiting.

Sabrina, do you want to tell them?

Yes, she replied as she looked at me and smiled.

Mami, grandma I asked Asia to marry me and she said yes.

I raised my hand to show off my engagement ring. Their faces just lit up, eyes teared up and they just smiled.

Maria walked over to me kissed me and gave me a hug.

Asia I am so happy for you both I am so happy that you and Sabrina will be able to share a life of love with each other.

Thanks ma, I replied.

My grandmother walked over to me kissed me, gave me a hug and said;

I am so happy for you both. Remember I always told you that if a love is true, it will always come back to you. Now you have the love of your life for life.

Thanks, you both. I am so happy I have the love of my life by my side and our family around us.

Asia, can I tell you something? Ma asked.

Yes, ma'am.

Do you remember that night you went to tell Sabrina how you felt about her right before graduation?

Yes, ma'am.

The next day she asked me to take her to the jewelry store to pick out a ring. The ring was for you. Sabrina sat me and grandma down and told us that she wanted to marry you. We all went together and picked out your ring. Yes, she was with Marcus but her heart has always been with you. She paid on that ring until she paid it off. She asked us never to say anything to you because she needed to figure this out for herself.

She also knew that if you knew at that moment it would confuse her even more. She had to find the truth about who she was in order to be the best wife she could be for the one she was destined to be with. I glanced over at Sabrina with tears in her eyes. I gently kissed her on her lips and held her close.

Her mother continued to speak.

Asia, you were always Sabrina's heart. But her struggles, she had to overcome them before she could be her best self.

Ma, I never would have guessed that. I knew Sabrina loved me and I loved her but I never thought she would be able to love me enough and be my wife.

Asia, baby that was her hardest struggle. She didn't know how to tell the family or even if she could. There were many days we sat and talked while she cried from her internal struggles. She even spoke with grandma some days when you thought she was out with Marcus. This was never easy for her. Once everything came to a head at the wedding her grandmother, aunts and uncles asked her why was this happening. She had to be open and honest. In her being open and honest she found out that if she would have just been honest with everyone, she would have been able to tell you how she truly felt and propose to you then. It was always you who had her heart.

Ma, thank you for telling me. I think everyone here knows that I would have waited until the end of time for Sabrina. I love her just that much. She is my twin flame, my soulmate, my air and life. To be honest I am grateful that this happened so we both can know that this is real and not just a passing phase.

I looked at Sabrina with so much love in my eyes. I kissed her on the forehead and held her hands. This has truly been a whirlwind but I look forward to the calm seas. There will be more discussions and things we must deal with. I look forward to the day I can call you, my wife. We all just sat there talking for a while and just enjoying each other. The fact that we were able to sit down and communicate made things better. If we can't be honest with ourselves, how can we be honest with others.

My prayers have been answered but it was a journey getting to this point.

By the way.

Sabrina, my love what type of wedding will you want?

Baby, whatever wedding with you as my bride. She leaned over and kissed me wrapped my arms around her and laid her head on my chest.

My love how about a small intimate beach wedding with family and a few friends?

Asia, I would love that.

Great, I will plan the whole thing, now that I have some experience with it. We all laughed. I have been saving ever since the day I met you, Sabrina.

How about April 10th? The day we first met.

I would love that, Asia. There are still a few things we need to work past but I know neither one of us are going anywhere. We have a lifetime to get it right. As we live life with no regrets.

No Regrets

"No Regrets"

"No Regrets"

By
Monya Williams

About the Author

Monya Williams was born and raised in Jacksonville, Florida. Blessed with the gift of storytelling she captures her readers with her colorful wordplay and passion. Monya uses the gift of telling stories in efforts to help one heal, move forward and keep pressing forward in the face of adversity. We all have a story to tell but many won't because we feel alone or may feel ashamed. Monya's goal is to show others they are not alone and they can overcome their biggest challenges if you keep the faith. Trust the process and know this too shall pass.

<u>Books by - Monya Williams</u>

Poetically Speaking

Crying Hearts

Love, Lust or Lies

My Eyes Saw More Than My Heart Can Handle

Words of My Pen

Picking up the pieces

The Soul of a Poet

Contact

Facebook: Monya Williams

Twitter: @Monya_Williams

Instagram: @therealmonya

Website: www.monyalwilliams.com

Made in United States
North Haven, CT
09 January 2022

14496430R00105